"The countdown is starting..."

It had already begun, Lindsey thought. It had started ten long years ago, and now it came down to this moment.

Three, two, one...

She went up on tiptoe, wrapped her arms around Carter's neck and met his mouth with hers.

His hands on her waist tightened as he drew her closer into the curve of his body. His chest was firm against hers. Solid. He held her as if he wasn't going to let her fall. Let her crash. And that was exactly what she needed.

Her pulse was racing, and little tingles were shooting down her body. Turning slightly, he moved them a few steps off the dance floor.

She felt the hard wall at her back and the warmth of Carter's skin through his shirt as he pulled her closer.

She needed more. So much more from him at this moment.

"Want to get out of here?" he asked.

She nodded. Tonight, she was impulsive...

Dear Reader,

Happy New Year! Do you make resolutions? I do. I'm shameless in my love of making lists and then working until I can check them off. Lindsey hasn't had the best year, and she's determined to make this new one count. She's starting over after a career-ending injury, and honestly, the last person she really wants to see is hotshot snowboarder Carter Shaw. But he's been flirting with her for forever, and she's tired of denying herself. Hey, it's New Year's Eve, so why not, right?

Of course, those kinds of decisions always have consequences, and one of them is the fact that Lindsey actually likes Carter more than she expected. And he's way more into her than a playboy should be.

I hope you'll enjoy this conclusion to the Holiday Heat series.

Happy reading!

Katherine

Katherine Garbera

After Midnight

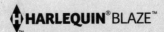

Recycling programs
for this product may
not exist in your area.

ISBN-13: 978-0-373-79834-6

After Midnight

Copyright © 2015 by Katherine Garbera

Printed in U.S.A.

™ www.Harlequin.com

Katherine Garbera is a *USA TODAY* bestselling author of more than fifty books and has always believed in happy endings. She lives in England with her husband, children and their pampered pet, Godiva. Visit Katherine on the web at katherinegarbera.com, or catch up with her on Facebook and Twitter.

This one is for Nancy Thompson and Mary Louise Wells. Thank you for the gift of your friendship.

1

"HELLO, GORGEOUS."

Carter Shaw.

Bad boy, snowboarder and Lindsey Collins' worst nightmare. Carter was everything she wasn't, and if she was being totally honest, everything she sort of wished she could be.

"Hello, trouble."

He laughed in that husky deep-throated way of his.

She tried to ignore the fact that his eyes were a kind of blue-gray that reminded her of early mornings on the slope just after the sun came up. His dark hair was thick and curly on the top, but at this moment cut short on the back of his neck. She'd seen him wear it a lot longer, but this sportier cut called even more attention to his handsome, gorgeous face. He had that sexy stubble that made her fingers tingle with the urge to touch it each time she saw him. And it didn't help her libido that the guy had that relaxed vibe of someone who'd grown up in California. To her, he'd always looked as if he should be on a surfboard instead of a snowboard.

"Nice shindig," he said. "If you like glamour."

Briefly glancing away to check out their surround-
ings, she smiled despite herself. The club at the Lars
Usten Resort and Spa certainly did New Year's Eve in
a big way. Lots of champagne. Lots of partygoers. Hats
and horns for everyone. There was a large dance floor
in the middle and banquettes around the end, as well as
lots of high tables.

"I can do glamour," she replied.

"You sure can," he said with a wink.

"Are you hitting on me?" she asked. "You've always
said you'd rather kiss your snowboard than a Super G
skier."

"Well, you are looking a lot better than my snowboard at the moment."

Lindsey shook her head at the way he said it. There
was something different about him tonight. He wasn't
his usual cocky self. They were both here this evening
because of the wedding of their two friends, Elizabeth
and Bradley. The newlyweds had long since departed
and she had stayed behind because it seemed a little too
Bridget Jones to be sitting all alone in her barely fur-
nished condo on New Year's Eve.

Up till now Lindsey had never been a big fan of staying up until midnight on New Year's Eve. What was the
point? Her entire life had been spent training to win an
international gold medal—and kissing someone at midnight really kind of paled in comparison to that goal. Or
at least it had. But tonight…she felt a little wild. A little
out of control. And if she was being completely honest,
she felt like doing something she'd never do otherwise.
Last year was supposed to have been *her* year, and she'd
crashed and burned playing by the rules and following
her plan. She'd suffered a humiliating fall in a practice

run in Sochi that had ended her career and changed her life. Instead of attacking the changes with her customary gusto, she'd settled into a sort of limbo here in Park City, Utah, at the Lars Usten lodge.

It had been so easy to do. The resort was cushy; her students at the lodge were cute and undemanding. The past six months or so had given her the chance to take it easy and slowly recover from more than knee surgery.

But this year... Well, this year all bets were off. Starting right here right now. The band was playing Van Morrison's signature hit, and she shot Carter a brazen look. "This is my song."

"Your song?"

She pointed to her eyes. Oh, God, was she really doing this? "'Brown Eyed Girl.'"

Yes, it seemed she was.

"Then let's dance," he said, grabbing her wrist and leading her onto the dance floor. He swung her around to face him, and she let go and pretended she didn't know all the things she knew about Carter.

That he played fast and loose with life and women. That he was a rebel risk taker who had caused more than one accident on the slopes. That he liked to put his hand on her hip and hold her close while they danced.

And he smelled good. A clean, crisp scent that reminded her of being outside and on the slopes.

She turned away from him.

She wasn't herself tonight. She should dance off the dance floor and out the door. Go home and forget about trying to be something and someone she wasn't.

Except she was lost.

Really lost...and she needed something to make her feel alive again. Something that going sixty miles per hour down the side of a mountain used to do but couldn't anymore.

"Gorgeous? You okay?"

No. Definitely *not* okay, but confessing that to Carter wasn't something she was going to do.

"Just thirsty."

"Let me get you a drink. Grab us some seats and we can chat."

"What would we possibly have to chat about?" she asked. "The charity event to get kids skiing that we're both working on. I know that's not until next November, but we are both playing a key role in it." His eyes gleamed with mischief. "*Or* the fact that, come midnight, I'm going to kiss you. I'll let you pick."

Suddenly tongue-tied, she watched him turn away and slowly weave his way through the crowd. He was popular, and everyone stopped him to chat or snap a quick selfie. And he smiled and acted as though he enjoyed it.

Heck, he probably did. She'd heard her coach say he loved the spotlight and the spotlight loved him. And she'd never seen any evidence to the contrary. How did he do it?

She wished there was some way she could claim his confidence for herself. To make herself into the invincible badass that Carter was. But the truth was she wasn't that type of girl, and no matter how much she tried, she wasn't going to change overnight.

Part of the problem was that she'd just come from an incredibly romantic winter wedding that seemed to emphasize that she was alone. Added to that, the bride's maid of honor, Penny, had recently hooked up with Will, her handsome vacation fling, which was quickly turning into something that was bound to last a lot longer.

And she was alone.

Lonely.

Desperate...

No. Not desperate. Though it did feel that way until Carter came back with a lemon-drop martini for her and some kind of mixed drink for himself. He slid in next to her at the high table instead of across from her and draped his arm along the back of the seat.

He canted his body toward hers and she thought, *What the hell.* She wasn't going to start another year the way she had all the rest. This year was going to be different, and Carter Shaw would be hers tonight.

CARTER HAD WANTED Lindsey since the first time he'd seen her. They'd both been two hotshot seventeen-year-olds being interviewed on ESPN, and when she'd looked straight at him with her pretty chocolate-brown eyes, he'd felt that spark shoot through his body.

But she'd always been the ultimate ice queen. Too cool for someone as wild and risky as he'd always been. But he'd gotten to know her better now. More than ten years later, he still wanted her, but he saw her through the eyes of a man and not a lusty boy.

Though, in all honesty, gazing at her now, looking like a gorgeous goddess, she still made him horny as hell.

And it was New Year's Eve. He'd spent more of them than he wanted to admit higher than the Rocky Mountains and with people whose names he couldn't recall.

He knew he'd changed over the course of the past year. The winter games had given him a check in the last box of his goals list. And it had been a sobering wake-up call when he'd witnessed Lindsey crash and realized his Nordic angel had feet of clay. Seeing her career end so quickly and unexpectedly had made him understand that he needed to look at his own life. He wasn't going to be able to snowboard forever at the top level of his event.

So he'd come here to Park City… Okay, in part to be closer to her. To see if maybe she'd be interested in him now that she wasn't so focused on training 24/7. But she still looked straight through him, as if he was just another man in the room. He wanted to be the *only* man in the room she saw.

Especially tonight.

"So, gorgeous, have you been thinking about that kiss?" he asked smoothly.

He sure had. It was hard to think of anything else when he was standing so close to her. Tonight she had her long, pale hair pulled back into an elegant updo. Tendrils framed her heart-shaped face and accentuated her long neck. Her mouth was full and sensuous, and she'd coated it with a sparkly lip gloss, which made it so hard for him to tear his gaze away. He leaned in closer. Almost kissed her before he pulled back.

He was waiting for midnight.

Besides, he had more control than that. He didn't give in to his baser instincts. Not anymore.

"I can tell it's been on *your* mind," she purred, lifting her hand and running her finger over his lower lip, back and forth, before spreading her fingers out and rubbing them over the stubble on his jaw.

She closed her eyes as she touched him for just a second, nibbling at her bottom lip before her hand dropped away.

"I have. You know I've been interested in you forever."

"Forever?" she said. "That's a bit of an exaggeration."

Not really. But admitting to her that she'd been his obsession for the better part of ten years wasn't something he planned to do tonight.

The band had switched to contemporary dance hits, and the loud, infectious beat pumped through the room. Lindsey swayed to it as she took a sip of her lemon-drop martini. It was sad that he knew what she liked to drink. But in a way she'd always been his safe fantasy. The one thing in his life, however distant, that was good and always just out of reach.

Until now.

He wrapped a wispy tendril of straight blond hair that was hanging along the nape of her neck around his finger. Her locks were exquisitely soft. Her skin, showed off by the stunning emerald-green dress she wore, so pale and creamy.

"Not an exaggeration. When we met at ESPN, I knew I wanted to kiss you."

She pursed her lips and tipped her head subtly away from him. "You were a player even then. And we both know you were attempting to throw me off my game. I almost let you."

"Why didn't you?"

"My parents. They had sacrificed a lot for me to get where I was, and no hotshot snowboarder with a tattoo was going to change that."

"*With a tattoo.* Is this a mark against me?" he asked, rubbing the side of his neck at the site of his first tattoo. It was a courage symbol that he'd seen in Japan when his father, an international businessman, had taken him there for a trip. Carter had been sixteen at the time and had snowboarded in Nagano while his father had worked. The tattoo had been his way of getting his father's attention while also proving to himself that he hadn't needed it. What could he say? He'd been a teenager.

She traced the design with her long, sparkly painted fingernail. "Not now. But back then you seemed wild and reckless. Too much for me. I needed to concentrate on my skiing."

"You were the fast one," he said with a wink. He knew that a lot of people thought what he did was dangerous—the flips and the 360s—but Lindsey had thrown her body down the mountain at speeds in excess of sixty miles per hour. Something that never failed to turn him on.

She scraped her finger down the column of his neck, sending delicious shivers through his body, and his cock stirred. Seeing his reaction, she leaned in closer, closed her eyes and released a sigh.

"Why is it that you are always racing ahead of me, then?" she asked in a soft whisper spoken right in his ear.

His ability to think was gone. Her breath was warm and her finger kept stroking his neck. All he could think about was her mouth. And how close it was to his. He turned his head to kiss her. Needed to feel her lips under his. But a waitress bumped into their table, jostling the drinks, and Lindsey pulled back.

Carter cursed under his breath but put on a smile for the cocktail waitress, who looked stricken. "No worries."

"These are for you," she said, setting down two cards and handing them Lars Usten Resort and Spa pens before walking away.

IT WAS ONE THING to decide she was going to spend the night with Carter, but she was finding it altogether more unnerving than she would have expected. In movies she'd seen the woman go after the guy, and then there would be a montage of kisses or dancing that ended up with the couple in bed. But she'd always been awkward at this stage.

There was something about Carter that for her was irresistible. His tattoo had fascinated her for a long time, and that stubble of his was just as a soft as she'd imagined it would be. She was letting the martini power her courage tonight…and she had to admit she liked it.

A lot.

"What is this?" She pulled the card the waitress had dropped on their table toward her. He'd been about to kiss her, and though she wanted that kiss, she was glad for the reprieve. She only needed a kiss at midnight. Not a public make-out session before that.

"Some sort of resolutions form," he said. "So, gorgeous, what do you want for this New Year?"

She arched a brow. "Why do you keep calling me that?"

"Because you are gorgeous," he said with another sly wink. "Plus, I'm sort of afraid if I say your name, you'll remember you don't like me."

"Ah, I wouldn't say I don't *like* you," she demurred. He was a little too wild and too out of control to be someone she felt comfortable with most of the time, but tonight that appealed to her. She wanted to forget who she was. Forget the past year had happened and wake up on January 1 as someone else.

That was pitiful, she thought. She should stop drinking. She'd had two martinis, and while she wasn't drunk, she did have that nice little buzz. But it was the maudlin thoughts that bothered her.

"Okay. What would you say about me, then?"

"I like that tattoo," she admitted. "And your stubble. How do you get it so soft?"

He laughed. "I've got more tattoos if you like that one."

"You do?" she asked. "Where?"

"I'll show you if you play your cards right."

She flushed a little. Not as bold as she wanted to be, but she wasn't backing away. She *was* doing this. She was going to be impulsive. And daring. Not Lindsey-like.

Needing a distraction, she glanced down at the resolution list on the card. "Do you do resolutions?"

"Seriously?" he asked with a mocking look. "Do I look like someone who wants to better myself?"

She shook her head, but realized in that instant that he was playing at being the bad-boy snowboarder she'd always thought he was. "I'm not sure about that. I think there is a big part of Carter Shaw the world never gets to see."

He shook his head. "Nah. I mean, there are those tattoos, but otherwise, what you see is what you get."

She doubted that. She was on to him. Why did he work so hard to be something he wasn't? For that matter, why did *she*? Because it was easier than letting the world see who she truly was.

"What food do you want to try next year?" she asked, reading from the list and hoping that she could keep her courage until midnight. Only another fifteen minutes. She wanted him. She wanted this New Year's Eve to be different from all the rest.

"Food, eh?" He wrinkled his forehead. "Not sure. I'm going with one of my cousins on a trip in Iceland to see a reindeer farm. So maybe reindeer?"

"I bet it doesn't taste like chicken," she said with a half smile. "When is that trip?"

"In the fall. It's a Northern Lights trip. We spend three weeks up close to the Arctic Circle living with the locals and watching each night for the aurora borealis."

That sounded…cold, but intriguing. "Have you done anything like that before?"

"Nah. This is the first year that I'm not competing anymore."

She looked at him in surprise. "What? Why not?" If not for her reconstructed knee, she'd still be training and focusing on four years from now. The next winter games.

"I have gold medals and more titles that one man could ask for. It's time to set my sights on something else."

"Such as…?" she asked, leaning closer. This is what she was searching for. *What* came after competing the way they had for most of their life? It was different for Carter because he'd been born with a silver spoon in his mouth. A little rich kid who got whatever he wanted. But that had only carried him so far. She knew that he'd worked as hard as she had to get to the winter games.

"Not sure. But this is my year of adventure. My year to find out. I'm working on that charity you're involved with to help kids get started in winter sports, because that's new for me. The old man is glad to see me giving back. Can you believe he said that to me?" Carter scowled. "I've given back a lot over the years."

For a moment she caught a glimpse of the real Carter.

"You have. I've heard about the board you developed. It changed snowboarding."

"Yeah, that was nothing," he said, flashing a grin at her. And the real man disappeared behind that flirty facade. "So what new food are you going to try?"

"Nothing exotic like you. I have a thing about dairy and have usually not eaten cheese. I know that sounds silly but this year I think I'll give it a try."

He lifted a brow. "Cheese?"

"Yes."

"You seriously don't eat cheese?" he asked.

She had friends who acted the same way when she mentioned it. "I don't like dairy stuff usually."

"Cheeseburgers?"

"Nope."

"Pizza?" he prodded.

"Pesto-based pizza with fresh tomatoes. No cheese."

"Weirdo," he said.

"Like *you're* normal!"

"Who wants to be normal?" he scoffed. "Okay…all kidding aside, what new thing are you really going to try?"

She looked at him for a long minute before the two lemon-drop martinis and her courage finally caught up with her mouth. "You."

2

"ME?"

"Yes, you. Remember all those times you badgered me for a kiss?" she asked.

He did. It had been a game for him since that first meeting. He'd wanted her, but she was out of his league. A classy woman—even at seventeen—who wouldn't give him a second glance. Of course, that hadn't stopped him. He'd teased her relentlessly, invaded her personal space and kept clamoring for a kiss.

"The last time I asked I thought I spooked you," he said, getting to the heart of the reason why he was really sitting with Lindsey Collins, who, despite her request for a kiss, would more than likely not end up in his bed this evening. He'd pushed her in Sochi. Had goaded her into agreeing that she'd kiss him if he beat his world-record time, and still she hadn't.

Not that he'd ever really expected her to fulfill her end of the bargain.

To him it had seemed like a simple little bet. Something to push her, because it had been ten years of flirting and it had seemed ridiculous to continue playing that game. And he'd been feeling trapped by his coach and sponsors, who'd wanted him to sign a new deal to keep doing the same thing he'd always done. So instead of acting like a man, he'd done what he always did and sought out Lindsey before her run to demand what he'd always wanted from her.

"It wasn't you. God, please, don't think that crash had anything to do with you," she said, reaching over to put her hand on his.

She leaned in, and the scent of her perfume filled the air around him. Her brown eyes were sincere as they met his. She squeezed his hand. "My crash was… I'm not sure what, but it wasn't you. I've been over the footage a million times. I wish that was an exaggeration, but it's not. I've watched it over and over again, trying to figure out what I could have done differently. Did you see how smooth I was at the top?"

"I did." He'd watched her run like everyone else. But for him, he'd felt that sense of pride he always did in her. He'd thought this time she'd beat him, and maybe that would put an end to his pursuit of her. Because she'd told him if she won that was the end of his kissing taunts.

But instead she'd crashed midway through her run. Her body and skis tumbling over each other. His heart had stopped beating for a second. She'd looked small and fragile as she'd crashed into the bright orange safety webbing. Guilt and fear had warred inside him.

"Well, it wasn't you. I think I hit the snow wrong out of the gate. My coach has a couple of theories, as well. But, honestly, I'm not so scared of being kissed that I'd crash.

"Kissed lots of guys, have you?"

She made a face. "A lady doesn't tell."

"Apologies."

"But I don't mind telling you that the anticipation with you has been killing me. I want to believe when you do kiss me it will be spectacular. However, given that it's been ten years of waiting, I can't rule out the possibility that it might be a dud."

He laughed. Threw his head back and just forgot everything else in this moment except for Lindsey. She was as nutty as he was but just covered it up better.

"It might. Or it could be the best damned thing either of us ever experiences."

She let go of his hand and settled back against the seat. "I guess that's why I've made you my resolution."

There was something different about her tonight. The wedding earlier had made him start thinking about things that he usually ignored. That and the fact that beginning tomorrow he was no longer only an athlete. He didn't have to train every day; he was going to chart a new path.

"Champagne or sparkling grape juice?" the cocktail waitress asked as she approached their table with a tray of drinks.

The Lars Usten Resort knew the party was going strong. Behind her was another waitress with hats with the year marked out in glitter and some kind of horn.

"Juice for me," Carter said. He didn't want to dull a single moment of the night with Lindsey, and although he liked to believe he could handle whatever life had thrown at him, he did it better when he was sober.

"Juice?" Lindsey asked, arching one eyebrow. "Champagne for me."

The waitress set their drinks in front of them, and then they were each given a hat. For him a top hat. For her a tiara. She promptly put it on her head and turned to bat her eyelashes at him. "Do I look like a princess now?"

"The queen should be afraid you're after her title," he murmured.

"As if. I'm not after anything. You're lucky, Carter. Lucky that you still have snowboarding. Life is very strange when you don't have to get up every day and train," she said, taking a sip of her champagne.

Not exactly what he'd been hoping to hear. "I think you're supposed to wait for the toast to drink that."

She smiled mischievously. "Going to tell on me?"

He shook his head. "Your secret's safe with me, Linds." How could he possibly deny this woman anything? She enchanted him. And he had to admit, she was a total mystery. He'd teased and cajoled her for his own amusement but had never really taken the time to get to know her. Tonight was showing him that all the preconceived notions he'd had were wrong.

She wasn't the ice queen she'd always been on the snow. She was real and fragile and so damned tempting...

LINDSEY HAD NEVER worn a tiara before. Even though this one was plastic with fake gems, she was still thrilled to be wearing it. It made her feel girlie. "This is my first real New Year's Eve party. Pitiful, isn't it?"

"Not really. Your life was focused in a different direction."

"Yeah, but you were training and still found time to party," she said.

"I'm good at multitasking," he replied.

"Most men really aren't."

He gave her a cynical look. "Really? You want to do the whole 'battle of the sexes' thing? Tonight?"

She didn't. She wanted to enjoy the fact that she felt like a normal girl instead of someone apart from the mainstream. The Ice Queen, the media had labeled her. But the truth was, she had gotten so used to keeping her feelings hidden it was hard for her to actually show them.

"Of course not. I had no idea your ego was so thin," she teased.

"It's not. But you should know if you throw down what you're going up against."

"What? That you're the boss?" she asked, trying not to smile. Carter had been flouting rules and tradition since the moment she'd met him. She found it really hard to believe that he'd have some hard set-in-stone ideas about anything. But she did believe that if he got into a fight, he'd go full-out and leave nothing.

She was used to winning and knew how to get what she wanted on the slopes but, one-on-one, she had a gut feeling he'd beat her every time. Hard as it was to admit, she just didn't know how to play a game like this.

She sighed.

Who was she trying to kid here? She wasn't going to be any different in the New Year than she'd been before. When had she ever been anything other than a stick-in-the-mud, tall, outdoorsy girl who would rather talk about skiing than anything else? Even her own family found her boring at times. Though they were kind about it and would listen to her talk about a new position or when she liked to shift her weight, she'd known they probably weren't really all that interested.

"Want to dance?" Carter asked, bringing her back

to the present. "One last spin around the dance floor to ring out the old year."

She nodded. "I'd like that. And *I'm* kissing *you* at midnight."

"Should I be on guard?" he murmured, stepping down from the high table and offering her his hand.

She took it and stumbled a little in her high heels. Bracing one hand on his chest, she whispered, "Not really. I know you want to kiss me."

His blue-gray gaze slowly drifted over her lips before he locked eyes with her once again. "I'm having performance anxiety now that you mentioned it. It might not be that great."

"I doubt that," she said. "You never have that."

"I wish I was as confident as you seem to think I am."

"Aren't you?" she breathed, reveling once again in his brisk masculine scent. They were pressed close together due to the crowds streaming in to hear the last song of the year. "You walked into a boardroom filled with executives you ticked off by campaigning to make them let you snowboard on their slopes, and then convinced them to back your charity event. You've got *nerve*, Shaw."

He had more than that. He seemed to embrace his life in a way she only had when she'd left the gate and started down the slope. She knew people thought what she'd done was dangerous, but to her it had just felt natural. It was a tightly controlled run down the mountain, and she'd spent her lifetime training. So she didn't credit that for anything other than being something she was good at.

She wanted to throw herself out of the gate of life, too. But she was getting a little nervous now that midnight was approaching. Carter had kissed lots of women; she knew that for a fact from all the gossip in the athlete's village at the winter games, and from firsthand accounts from other Alpine skiers over the years. As for her... Well, she hadn't kissed that many men. And the few sexual encounters she'd had were hurried affairs that had left her feeling cold and wanting more.

She didn't want Carter to be the same. She'd sort of set him on the sex-god pedestal in her mind a long time ago. *What if he wasn't?*

Or worse yet, what if he was great and she was the dud?

Ugh! This was what happened when she stepped outside her nice, safe, little zone. Carter stared down at her with those intense eyes of his, and she hoped she looked intriguing or inviting but was afraid she might just seem confused.

"What?"

"We don't have to dance," he said softly.

"I want to." She had in her head an image of New Year's Eve, and it involved her looking glamorous, which, thanks to the beautiful dress she wore, ticked that box. And she had a very handsome, sexy man who'd just asked her to dance.

She took his hand in hers. It would be too much for the band to play "The Way You Look Tonight," but in her mind she wanted them to. Instead they danced to "Wrecking Ball." Something that didn't speak well for love.

But this wasn't about love.

This thing between her and Carter had always been about pure lust. And tonight she was finally going to cross the finish line. Get the kiss he'd been taunting her with since they'd met.

The funny thing was, she was just as scared about that today as she had been when she was seventeen. He held her close, and for just a second she rested her head on his strong shoulder. Pretended they were that couple in her mind. The couple who could gaze lovingly into each other's eyes at midnight and share a kiss so profound it would rock both their worlds.

But then Carter squeezed her hip and slid his hand up the middle of her back.

She tipped her head back to look up at him.

"The countdown is starting."

It had already begun, Lindsey thought. It had started ten long years ago, and now it came down to this moment.

She licked her lips and couldn't help but focus on his mouth. Those chiseled, full lips nestled in that closely shorn stubble.

"Ten. Nine. Eight. Seven. Six. Five…"

"Ready?"

"Three. Two. One."

She went up on tiptoe, wrapped her arms around his neck and met his mouth with hers. His lips were soft, surprising her into parting hers. His breath was warm and minty, and he held her loosely, but she was rooted to the spot.

Around her people were kissing and celebrating, but her world had narrowed to just Carter. *Carter Shaw.*

Of course, he kissed like a dream. He was the kind of man who'd had lots of practice, but this didn't feel routine, like something he'd done a million times before. To her it felt special and it awakened the passion she'd tucked away after her crash. It felt as though she was finally able to relax again as he kissed her.

She held his shoulders, and his hands on her waist

tightened as he pulled her closer into the curve of his body. His chest was firm against hers. Solid. He held her as if he wasn't going to let her fall. Or let her crash. And that was exactly what she needed.

She framed his face with her hands. Ran her fingers over that soft stubble of his and then pulled back. But he followed her. Kissing her again, dropping soft and tantalizing kisses along the line of her jaw before he lifted his head to look down at her.

"Not a dud," he said.

"Not at all. That was…"

"Unexpected?" he suggested in a smooth, sexy voice.

His hands on her waist caressed her. She noticed that as the music changed to "Auld Lang Syne" and he pulled her closer, swayed with her to the music. She didn't want him to let go. Maybe it was the drinks she'd had tonight or the fact that this was a new year. A new slate for her. But something made this moment with Carter seem almost perfect.

The rational part of her brain tried to say it wasn't, but she shushed it. For just one night she wanted to be like every other person and not analyze her actions to death. She wanted to live.

She grabbed Carter's shoulders and pulled him toward her. Caught his mouth with hers and kissed him the way she'd seen it done in the movies. The way she'd tried in the past. She'd found reality and movie kisses didn't deliver in the same way; they'd always ended up tasting not quite right. But this time, as her tongue slid past his lips and into his mouth, everything felt different. Carter tasted good. His kiss was warm and…yes, perfect. Absolutely, profoundly perfect. He leaned over her and bent her back the slightest bit, angling his head to deepen the kiss. Her pulse was racing, and little tingles shot down her body. He twisted and moved them a few steps off the dance floor.

She felt the hard wall at her back and Carter's warmth pressed into her. He pulled his mouth from hers, but only went as far as her neck, where he suckled at the skin as his hands roamed up and down her body.

She skimmed her own hands down the strong muscles of his back to his lean hips and tugged him closer. Felt the shaft of his erection against her and knew he wanted more.

She needed more. So much more from him at this moment.

"Want to get out of here?" she asked.

"I've got a room at the lodge." He exhaled roughly. "Is that what you want?"

She nodded.

She didn't want to talk about it or to discuss it too much or she might change her mind.

And tonight she was being impulsive.

"Yes, I want you."

"I want you, too. I have for a long time," he said, taking her hand and leading her out of the dance club. The lobby was quiet, almost shockingly so after the noise in the club. But there were a few staff members who smiled at them and wished them a happy New Year.

She kept her hand laced tightly with Carter's; trusted him to lead her through this night. This new beginning. The one she'd wanted for so long but hadn't been sure how to find.

They were alone in the elevator car, and Carter dropped her hand and stood a few inches from her. "Are you sure about this? I don't want you to have any regrets."

"I promise you I won't." That much she knew was true. She'd regret it more if she walked away from him. If she let this moment pass.

Suddenly she realized that it had been fear holding her here. Fear that had motivated everything she'd done since the crash. The crash that had taken her career and could have taken her life.

She'd been lucky.

Now she wanted to make up for lost time, wanted to make the most of her life, but had been struggling to get over the hump and actually do it.

Figured it would be Carter Shaw who'd push her and get her moving again.

She cupped his butt and squeezed. "Are you having doubts?"

He turned around, and she hadn't realized how turned on he was by her until that moment. He moved toward her, backed her up against the side of the elevator car and kissed her full-on, his entire body pressing provocatively against hers.

His chest rubbed over her breasts, his hips canted in toward her and she felt the brush of his erection at her center. His hands went to the back of her head as his mouth hungrily claimed hers. He kissed her with a long, deep kiss that left her trembling and wanting so much more.

The bell dinged and the elevator doors slid open. But still he kissed her as if he couldn't let her go. The doors started to slide shut, and he pulled back and cursed. He shoved his foot out to stop them from closing and tugged her behind him as he stepped into the hallway.

"I'm not changing my mind, gorgeous. I can promise you that."

3

CARTER LED HER into his suite. He'd left the light on over the bed because he had never been a fan of a dark room. Kissing Lindsey was like the first time he'd hopped in the half-pipe and had the ride of his life.

She'd awakened something inside him that was so much more than physical. It was easy to say the affection and lust roiling through him right now was due to the day he'd spent with her. They'd both been in the bridal party. Lindsey as a bridesmaid and Carter as a grooms-man. The other couple standing up for Elizabeth and Bradley was a real couple, so she and Carter had sort of been forced together. In spite of all his faults, he'd never been a big fan of lying, even to himself.

She cupped his butt again and groaned. He wanted to take this slow, but if she kept fondling him it was going to be a wham-bam-thank-you-ma'am encounter up against the wall of his hotel room.

Even the thought of that made him shiver. God, he wanted her.

"Want a drink?" he asked, forcing himself to take a few steps from her. He hoped the distance would clear his head and maybe penetrate the red haze of lust that was surrounding him. Make him remember he'd wanted her for a long time. Their first time should be epic.

"There is only one thing in this room that I want, Carter Shaw, and I'm looking straight at him."

She kicked off her high heels as she sauntered toward him, her hand under her arm. For a moment it looked as if she was cupping her own breast. He groaned as she slowly dragged her hand down the side of her own body. The dress gaped and he realized she was getting naked.

"Slow down, gorgeous, we have all night," he said, toeing off his shoes as she closed the distance he'd put between them.

"It's midnight, Carter, which means we only have six more hours until morning. Until the cold light of day. I don't want to waste a second of it."

She was different. He wanted to be, too. He wanted to just go with it and pretend that this was the real Lindsey. Except he knew it wasn't.

Was she playing a game tonight?

She placed her palm flat on his chest, and then leaned into him. The scent of her perfume once again surrounding him, inundating his senses. Pressing even closer, she went up on tiptoe to kiss his neck, just above his tattoo, as her hands pushed his jacket off his shoulders and down his arms.

He let the jacket fall to the floor, then slipped one of his hands into the gap in her unzipped dress. Her skin was cool and satiny smooth. He felt his way over her ribs toward her breasts. Her breath hitched, and she caught the lobe of his ear between her teeth and bit down lightly.

"I'm curious where those other tattoos of yours are,"

she said, her fingers moving between them and undoing the buttons at the front of his shirt.

Her breath brushed over his neck and made him throb even more. Shivers spread down his body; blood pooled in all the right places, making his skin sensitive and cock rock hard. He stopped thinking of how he wanted this to be and just followed her lead.

Lindsey wasn't going to let him put her off her goal. And as she'd said downstairs, her resolution for the year was him. He'd never been anyone's anything special before. Fun time, sure, but that wasn't all he intended to be for Lindsey tonight.

He pushed his hand farther into her dress, up her back, and found the clasp of her bra. Undoing it with one hand and then rubbing his hand between her shoulder blades, pulling her closer to him as he lowered his head to take her mouth with his.

She tasted like the promise of a night he'd never forget. Her mouth was both languid and passionate under his. Her tongue tangled against his in a slow, sensuous dance that felt as though it would never end. As though it didn't have to end tonight.

Her hands slid under his shirt, her fingers cool against the fabric of his T-shirt, and he felt the bite of her nails into his pecs. "Where is your skin? How am I going to see these rumored tattoos of I can't get to you?"

A laugh rumbled through him. "Sit on the bed."

"No."

"I thought you wanted to see me?"

"I do, but that doesn't mean you get to be bossy," she said.

Lindsey slipped her hands up over his shoulders again

and pushed his dress shirt down his arms. "You forgot my cuffs."

"No, I didn't," she drawled. "I think you'll see that you are trapped. And I am in charge."

He wasn't trapped at all. He might not have a full range of motion, but he could still hold on to her waist, which he did. But she stepped back and put her finger right in the center of his chest. "Why don't you go sit on the bed?"

He laughed again, that jolt of lust and joy taking him by surprise. And he did what she asked, slowly working his hands to free them as he sat. As soon as his hands were free, he leaned back on his elbows and arched one eyebrow as he looked over at her. "Okay, now what?"

"Hmm…let me see." She moved forward, straddled him on the bed and brought her mouth down hard on his. She sucked his tongue into her mouth, and everything inside him came to attention as she nipped his tongue and then abruptly stood. "Take off your T-shirt."

"Take off your dress. I'm dying to see what you look like without it."

"Can I keep my tiara on?" she asked impishly.

"Definitely. I think the Ice Queen should always wear her crown."

She stepped away, shimmied out of her dress and then let her bra slowly slide down her torso, pulling first one arm free and then the other and dangling it from one finger. She stood there with that cool Nordic beauty. His gorgeous ice queen, very sure of herself and her appeal.

He started to get up, but she wagged her finger at him. "Did I say you could move?"

"I think you're going to want me to move," he told her.

"Not yet."

He sank back on the bed and grimaced as his slacks cut into his erection. He shifted and then thought, *To hell with it,* and unzipped his pants, pushing them down his legs.

"You look good, Carter. You could be an underwear model."

He'd done a few ads in his day, but lately he preferred to keep some things for himself and his lovers. His body was one of them. He stood and slowly pulled the hem of his T-shirt up past his abdomen as he closed the gap between them. She reached out and traced the tattoo on his left side. Her fingers were warm and seeking as they moved over him.

The design disappeared into the top of his boxer briefs, and she pulled the elastic waistband away from his skin, pushing the side of the briefs down so she could see the entire thing.

"Is this a mountain?"

"Yes. Nagano."

"Why Nagano?"

He let out a groan. "*Now?* You want to talk now?" he asked, painfully aware that he could barely string together two words as she leaned lower to examine his ink. Her beautiful, lush breasts swayed forward and her breath brushed over his hip. She was so close to his cock, he could only think of twisting his hips so that he could feel her touch where he desired it most.

"I guess not. But later," she said, "I want to know more about it."

"Later," he growled, cupping her breasts, rubbing his palm over the center of her nipples and gently fondling them.

She caressed his upper body and pushed the T-shirt

up and over his head. He stopped stroking her as she tossed it aside. Again she put her hand in the center of his chest and pushed against him. He walked backward until he felt the edge of the bed at the back of his thighs, and put his arm around her waist, dragging her forward with him as he sat. Inhaling her sweet, womanly scent, he pulled her onto his lap so she straddled him.

She reached up and did something with her hair, letting it fall around her shoulders as she leaned forward. Staring at him with passion-glazed eyes, she cupped his face, rubbed her fingers through his short stubble and then leaned down to kiss him. Not a dominating one, as earlier, but one that promised that the games were over. He held her close to him with one hand on her hip, and let his other hand caress her, starting at the back of her neck and then slowly moving down the back of her spine. He felt her shiver as he traced his way around the tiny indentation right above her buttocks.

He caressed her hips, and she rocked forward against him, then winced. Her knee. He'd forgotten that she'd injured it a year ago. He scooted back on the bed and rolled them onto their sides so they were facing each other.

"Sorry," she whispered.

"Hey, gorgeous," he said, lightly running his hand down the side of her body over her curves. "It's okay. How's the knee?"

"Fine. It was just the angle."

"Then let's find a better angle," he suggested. "One where we don't have to think about anything but each other."

She nodded. But the confidence that had been driving her had waned. He could read it in her eyes. "I guess I'm in charge now."

Just as he suspected, the thought of the power shift was enough to nudge any embarrassment Lindsey had over her knee out of her subconscious. She gave him an arched look, raised herself up onto her elbow and put her finger to the middle of his chest again.

"Not so fast." She leaned over him, slowly following the pattern of his chest hair as it narrowed down his belly and disappeared into the top of his boxer briefs. Then she dipped her finger under the elastic and brushed the tip of his cock, and his hips jerked forward.

He breathed in and out, struggling to stay in control. Then he reached for her and mimicked her caress. He started in the middle of her chest and traced his finger down around each of her breasts, and then lower to her belly button. He drew a small circle around it and then leaned over to trace the path with his mouth. But he lingered at her breasts, catching her nipple in his mouth and sucking as he continued to fondle her belly button.

She pushed her hand into his underwear and slid her hand up and down his shaft. He shivered in response, felt as though he was going to lose it, but instead rocked himself against her touch. He liked it. Her fingers were long, and she wrapped them around his length, stroking up and down within the confines of his underwear.

He lifted his lips from her breast to move lower, kissing each of her ribs, and her hand slid off him as he did so. She let her fingers drift up his body and around to his back. Caressing the area near his tattoo, her fingers moved gently over the imprint as he tongued her belly button and then dipped his head lower. He peeled her underwear over her hips and down her long legs, stopping to kiss the scars at her knee, and then tossed them to the floor.

He shoved his own briefs off, ready to be totally naked.

"Are you on the pill?" he asked.

"What?" She seemed dazed, and he realized that he'd jarred her.

"Are you protected from pregnancy?"

She nodded. "Are you clean?"

Fair question, given his reputation, but still… "Yes. Are you?"

"Of course," she said.

"Good."

He moved so that he could take her ankles in his hands to raise her legs. He smiled as she propped herself up on her elbows.

She was spread out in front of him, her tousled blond hair falling around her shoulders, her pink-tipped breasts rising and falling with each breath she took. His eyes traced her nipped-in waist and the soft blond curls at the apex of her thighs. The long smooth legs that he'd admired often when she'd worn snow pants.

She had a great ass, but he'd save that for next time. Tonight was special. It was the first time, and he wanted it to be just right. Wanted to see her face, so that in his mind he'd always have this image of Lindsey.

Naked. Wanting. Completely his.

He brought her foot to his chest and caressed her leg, starting at the ankle and working his way to her thigh, stopping just short of her center. Then he did the same with her other leg, lingering over the scars on her fully healed knee. Next he used his mouth on the same path, and when he got to the apex of her thighs, she sighed and tangled her hands in his hair as he parted her and kissed her most intimate flesh.

She shifted under him, her heels pushing down on the bed as she lifted her hips toward his mouth. He flicked his tongue over her and then moved lower to taste her. She slipped her hands across his back, her nails digging into his shoulders as his mouth took full possession of her. Her thighs came up on either side of his face as she thrashed underneath him.

She tried to pull him up over her, but the taste of her was addicting and he couldn't get enough of it. His cock was hard and he wanted to be buried deep inside her, but he didn't want to have to stop tasting her, either.

He swirled his tongue around the little pink bud at the center of her and felt it swell under him. Her nails dug into his shoulders, and she made a breathy sort of moaning noise that let him know she liked it. He slipped his finger inside, stroking her. He kept it up until she tugged at his hair, and he lifted his head.

"Carter."

"Yes, gorgeous?"

"I want you inside me."

"I am inside you," he said.

She sighed and shifted on the bed, bending at the waist, finding his cock first with her hand and then with her mouth. He felt her tongue feather down the side of his shaft as her fingers lightly caressed his balls. She squeezed him as she took the tip of him inside her mouth, her tongue swirling all around it.

A drop left him, and he pulled back. This first time he wanted to come inside her body. Wanted to see her face as they both climaxed.

His hips jerked, and he realized that if she kept this up, he wasn't going to last at all. He pulled his hips back, sitting up and noticing the very satisfied look on her face. Evidently she'd gotten what she wanted. She was a minx, and seeing this side of her made him wonder what else he thought he knew about Lindsey that he didn't.

But he didn't mind, because he was getting what he wanted, too. He took her hands in his, stretching them above her head as he levered his body over hers, shifting his hips until he felt the opening of her body.

"Got your way," he rasped. "I hope you're ready for me."

"I am." She lifted her hips as she wrapped her legs around him, and he slid into her. She held him tight to her and moved her hips to bring him closer each time. Cupping his buttocks, she pulled him.

She was tight and felt so good that he drove all the way home and immediately pulled back to do it again. She wrapped her arms around his shoulders, lifting herself up to whisper hot words of need and desire in his ear. She told him how much she wanted him. How she needed him deeper and deeper.

And he did exactly what she asked. Drove himself into her again and again, deeper each time. He felt shivers run down his spine. Reached between them to caress her clit because he knew he wasn't going to make it much longer. He was going to come and he wanted— needed—to make sure she did, as well.

She moaned his name, bit his neck and arched her body frantically underneath him and then cried out. He felt her body tighten around him, her inner walls gripping his cock and urging him on. Pounding into her, harder and faster than before, he gazed down into those big chocolate-brown eyes as he felt his orgasm rush through him.

He emptied himself inside her and then collapsed,

careful to support his weight with his arms. He dragged one of his hands from where he'd held hers, caressing her arm and shoulder, and then rolled to his side, keeping their bodies joined as he cuddled her close.

She rested her head on his shoulder and ran her fingers over his chest. He felt each exhalation of her breath against her skin, and she sighed a little.

Did she regret this?

"I guess that proves it."

"Proves what, gorgeous?" he asked, almost afraid of her answer. He wanted to lie here with her in his arms and just pretend for a moment that he didn't have to let her go.

"That you're not a dud," she said.

4

HER BODY TINGLED, and she felt more alive than she had in the past year. She pushed herself from Carter and leaned back on her elbow so she could watch him. God, a man shouldn't look like this. Not when he was lying next to her in bed. He was all sinew and muscle and, despite his reputation for being debauched, he was in very good shape.

He'd said he was retiring from snowboarding but there was no evidence of that in his lean, hard body.

His eyes were half-closed; he had one hand on her waist, idly gliding up and down her side. His hands were large but sort of soft when he touched her. The confidence and the courage that had brought her up to his room and into his bed were still there. Buzzing around in her mind, which was a little fuzzy from the drinks she'd had and the sex.

God, she'd had no idea sex could be like that. Could be that good. She understood now why so many people were tempted to miss their training schedules for it.

"Was it a surprise for you?" she asked a bit tentatively. Maybe this was the way it always was for him.

He fully opened his eyes, turning his blue-gray gaze on her. "What?"

"The sex. Or is it always like that for you?"

"Damn, gorgeous, the things you ask," he said. Scrubbing a hand over his eyes, he grabbing a pillow from the head of the bed and bunched it up under his head.

"If I don't ask I'll never know. And you *are* a player," she reminded him.

He arched one dark eyebrow at her.

"Not going to try to deny it, are you? I heard about many of your hook-ups over the years."

"Why would I when you wouldn't believe me anyway?"

"I don't know. Actually, I really don't know you," she admitted. She traced the tattoo of Nagano on his hip. She'd skied there at a world-cup competition twice. She traced the path down his hip and noticed that he let her, just kept still while she ran her finger over his skin.

She didn't know what to do next. She hadn't been kidding when she'd said this wasn't her kind of situation. And let's face it, most etiquette books didn't cover what to do when a woman ended up in bed with a bad-boy snowboarder. In fact, her mom would have probably said don't end up there. She was practical like that.

He sat up and caught her hand in his, bringing it ever so slowly to his lips. He kissed her palm and then looked her straight in the eye. She saw the sincerity his gaze and something else. Something she couldn't really define.

He leaned closer. She closed her eyes because it felt too intense. The room smelled of sex and Carter. That spicy aftershave she'd noticed that lingered in the air after they'd had a conversation.

"It was special for me, too."

"Why do you think that is?" she asked, opening her eyes and almost smiling. She wanted to hear that she was different from the other women. Carter had exceeded her wildest expectations and made her realize that the safe dates and bed partners she'd had in the past weren't the norm.

He laughed again. "Give me a minute to wash up, and then we can continue this conversation."

He got out of the bed and padded naked to the bathroom, returning a moment later with a warm washcloth for her to use. He took it back into the bathroom, and while she was alone, she glanced around the room and caught a glimpse of herself in the mirror over the desk. She notice her tiara with the year on it on its side near the bed.

She placed it on the nightstand before scooting up and getting under the covers. As she leaned back against the headboard, she realized he might not want her to stay.

This would have been easier if she'd taken him to her place. Then she maybe she wouldn't feel so awkward.

He strode back into the room with all the grace and elegance of a tiger.

She forced a smile and what she liked to think of as her game face. The expression she used in the press room after a bad run, or when she'd had to go in front of the media and act as though it hadn't mattered that her career in skiing was over after her fall.

Watching his muscles moving with each step he took, she realized he was a perfect specimen. Not like her body, which was broken and bore fresh scars. She envied him his healthy body. Tamping down her roiling emotions, she shook her head. She wasn't going down that path tonight.

Instead, the sheet falling to her waist, she drank him in. "Dammit."

"What's wrong?" she asked in alarm.

"You make me want to start all over again."

"Start what?" She wasn't following him.

"Sex," he said. "I've just had you but I want you again. Want to take my time and make sure that I haven't missed one glorious spot on your body."

She arched one eyebrow at him. "I don't think you did. But first I want to hear why you think I'm special."

He rubbed a hand over his chest and came to sit next to her on the bed. "Gorgeous, you've always been special to me."

That was a nonanswer if she ever heard it, but it was New Year's Day. He was her little gift to start out a fabulous year, and she guessed from his tone that discussing their past wasn't exactly what he had in mind.

She sighed, but the drinks and her emotions were catching up with her. She traced his tattoo and thought of all the risks she'd taken in her life and how they'd paid off for her. Carter Shaw was the biggest one. She'd come to his room for a night of pleasure and hopefully to jar herself out of the sameness that her life had taken on.

That was it.

It was hard, though, because she was a planner, and to face any situation knowing that she didn't have a proved strategy made her edgy and scared.

IF SHE'D BEEN any other woman, he would have been happy to climb back into that bed and have another round of mind-numbing sex. But this was Lindsey. His gorgeous Nordic angel who'd always been different. And tonight was no exception.

She kept touching him in that innocent way of hers that turned him on, but more than that, she seemed to touch him as if she wasn't thinking about it.

"Tell me about this tattoo."

That she'd changed the subject kind of let him off the hook and also disappointed him the tiniest bit. He wanted her to demand some answers from him, not let him keep skating by on the surface. But she saw him the way every other woman did. She was different to him but he wasn't different to her.

It hurt for a split second before he shrugged it aside and shifted to lie next to her. He pulled a couple of pillows closer and propped them under his head.

"What about it?"

"When did you get it?"

"On a trip to Japan with my dad when I was a teenager."

"How on earth did you convince them to give you a tattoo…or did your dad okay it?" she asked with a smile.

Carter thought of his old man and how, back then, he'd been sort of his enemy. Now that he was an adult they got on well, but growing up, his dad had seemed like this guy who had never really lived or ever done anything daring. The exact opposite of everything that Carter wanted to be. His mom had died in childbirth, and his dad had never recovered.

"No, he didn't approve. But I was on my own, spoke decent Japanese and looked like I was eighteen. I knew from the moment I'd seen the mountain that I wanted it. I wanted to snowboard down it, learn its paths and twists and turns. Try to capture some of its wildness."

He lifted his head and stared down into her pretty

brown eyes. She smiled in response. "That's almost poetic. Watch it, Shaw, your badass image is slipping."

"I got ink at sixteen. That's pretty badass," he retorted, trying to push aside the feelings she called easily to the surface. He wasn't one of those guys who spent much time thinking heavy thoughts. So he could only blame Lindsey and this evening for stirring up those old memories.

"And now you're twenty-seven and retiring? Time flies, doesn't it?" she said, rolling onto her back and lifting her arms up above her head.

The movement forced her breasts into prominence, and he reached over and feathered his fingers across them. Slowly stroking her skin, which was very smooth and very warm. Addicting almost. He never wanted to stop touching her.

She turned over again, facing him. "I don't want to talk about the past."

"Me, either."

The present was way more interesting than the things he'd done in the past. For instance, this was the first time he was close enough to hold Lindsey in his arms. Close enough to notice that on her rib cage just below her breast she had a small birthmark. He leaned in to kiss it.

"What are you doing?"

"Memorizing you. Trying to make sure I know every inch of you."

"I thought it took guys a while to recover after sex," she said.

He shook his head and laughed. "Some guys. Some of the time. I think it depends on the woman and man. It's not taking me any time with you."

"Why do you think that is?" she asked curiously. "Is it back to me being special?"

He caressed her side, starting at her shoulder and working his way slowly down to her hip. "I don't know why. It's not something I've ever analyzed. Why would I? Sex is supposed to be fun, not figures put in a spreadsheet."

"Is it?" she mused. "That hasn't always been my experience, but then I haven't done the amount of experimenting you have."

"Gorgeous, you're pushing me. I'm not sure why."

"I'm scared," she admitted. "This seemed like fun in the bar, but now that I'm up here, I don't know how to act or what to do next. I'm not used to that."

He sighed. "There is no right or wrong action here. We make up our own rules, okay?"

He wanted her to be different, and she was. She made him feel alive in a way that only snowboarding had before. Something he'd never found in any of his personal relationships. Maybe it was just the novelty of sleeping with a girl he'd wanted since he was seventeen. Or maybe it was just the place he was in at this moment in his life.

But he didn't want her to think they had to behave in a certain way. With other woman he'd been different— happy for the sex, but not wanting anything more. It had been casual and friendly with no feelings getting hurt. But this was Lindsey, and he needed more.

More? How much more, he had no idea. This was all new to him, too.

"Okay, so what kind of rules should we have?" she asked. "Are we going to do this again?"

"Um…I thought that was obvious," he said, gesturing to his erection.

She laughed, and the sound washed over him like a warm bit of sunshine on a cold day.

A moment later she reached for him, stroked her hand up and down his cock, and then leaned down to kiss him. "Okay, so after that—then what?"

"We'll figure it out. This is one thing we don't have to train for or have a rigorous schedule about." She nodded, and he saw that something was going on inside her head, but he had no idea what it was. What was it she was thinking? He thought maybe he shouldn't let himself get distracted, but for tonight he'd had enough conversation.

He had a naked Lindsey in his bed and he intended to enjoy her.

THEY FELL ASLEEP in each other's arms after making love the second time, and when Lindsey woke, it was to the soft snores coming from Carter. He was turned on his side, facing her, and their fingers were linked together. She was riveted by the sight of him, but had a little bit of a headache and was thirsty.

Really thirsty.

She carefully pulled her hand from his and made her way quietly across the bedroom into the bathroom, where she closed the door, letting just the illumination from the night-light break the darkness. She saw herself in the mirror, but avoided eye contact as she filled a glass with water and slowly drank it.

Lost in thought, she closed the lid on the toilet and sat on it.

She was no closer now to knowing what to do next

than she had been six hours earlier. She noticed she had a little bit of razor burn on her neck, remembered the feel of him in her arms and shivered. Carter Shaw. Who'd have guessed?

She finished her water and then stood to lean in over the sink.

Her previous sexual experiences had been less than stellar. Did she look different now that she'd had an orgasm with a man rather than by her own hand? She searched her face for some sign, but there wasn't one. She still looked like Lindsey. Like herself. But inside something had awakened. Something was changing, and she had no clue what she was going to do next.

She bit her lip. Staying here and waiting for Carter to wake up sounded like a bad idea. She knew that last night was only one night. It had been fun and frivolous, two things she'd never embraced in her entire life. But she'd liked it. No regrets.

You only live once, right? But now it was a new day and time for making plans.

No matter how incredible it had been, there was no denying that this thing between her and Carter wasn't going to last. They had nothing in common aside from sports, and skiers and snowboarders were very different. Frankly, they didn't really even know each other that well.

Something that she intended to ensure didn't change. Because there was no need for it to. He was going back to his wandering ways, and though she'd cross paths with him once in a while on the committee for the charity event, she doubted she'd really see that much of him.

She felt a little pang and ignored it. Of course, the thought of going back to the adversarial strangers they'd been hurt after last night. After sharing something with him she'd experienced with no other man. But it wasn't going to happen again. Carter was a bad boy and not at all the kind of guy she was interested in trying to date. Besides, her life was a big-ass mess right now.

Lindsey sighed. Her clothes were scattered in the other room, and she needed to collect them, get dressed and beat a hasty retreat before he woke. But first she grabbed one of the robes from behind the door...because in the cold light of day walking around naked didn't feel right.

She opened the door cautiously and heard the low rumble of Carter's voice.

"Thank you very much."

He was awake.

He was sitting on the edge of the bed, his back to her, his brown hair tousled and sticking up a little on the left side. He tossed the cordless phone onto the bed and stood. "I ordered breakfast."

"I actually should probably be going," she said hastily. "I feel like I've—"

"Where do you have to go? I know you're not working today."

"You do?" Her eyes widened. "How do you know that?"

"Because you were drinking and partying last night. I know you aren't the type of person to ski after a night like that," he said. "Take it from me, your concentration won't be that great."

"Have you done that? Snowboarded in that condition?"

"I have. I don't recommend it." There was a long

pause. "Let me grab a robe and we can have breakfast, okay?"

She didn't want to get to know Carter any better. Sure, she knew how that sounded, but the truth was, the more she knew him the bigger the chance of her starting to like him was. She didn't want to change the dynamic between them that had worked so well for so long. She had figured out a way to manage him.

"I'm not sure."

"Really? *Now* you're running scared?" Crossing his arms over his bare chest, he flashed a taunting smile her way. "After all that we did to each other last night, this morning you want to retreat?"

She gave him the hardest stare she could muster. Given her headache she suspected it wasn't as steely as she'd like. "I'm not a child to be swayed by a petty dare."

"It wasn't petty, gorgeous. It was a flat-out challenge. Prove you're not a coward and stay."

She rolled her eyes. This was the guy she had no chance of ever falling for... The one who needled her and tried to make her— "Fine. I'll stay for breakfast."

He nodded. "I'll be right back."

She walked over to the table set up in a corner of the suite with chairs that faced the plate-glass windows that provided a perfect panoramic view of the Wasatch Range. The mountains she knew like the palm of her hand. She'd skied all the different runs down that mountain. It was a constant to her. In fact, she'd trained there for so long it was like her home.

But it wasn't anymore. And she knew that it wasn't Carter she was angry with this morning. It wasn't the mountain, either, although that big majestic thing did play a part in it. She was angry with herself. For falling and for failing. She'd never realized how much she'd let herself down. Hadn't wanted to admit that to herself. As a matter of fact, she hadn't been able to let those emotions out until this morning.

Coffee and breakfast weren't going to sweeten her mood now. *That* she understood, so she got dressed as quickly as she could, gathered her clutch and her tiara and walked out the door before Carter came out of the bathroom.

She needed time and distance. Not the distraction that he provided.

5

IT DIDN'T TAKE a Stephen Hawking–level genius to figure out that Lindsey wanted to be left alone. But Carter hadn't achieved all he had in the world of snowboarding, or in life, by not going after what he wanted. And after last night, it was pretty damned clear to him that he still wanted more from her.

He took a shower, got dressed, ate the breakfast he'd ordered and then went out to find her. She worked at the lodge, and he suspected she must live pretty close to it. They'd both been serious athletes for the majority of their lives—if Lindsey was anything like him, she'd want to be close enough to the mountains to spend all her free time on the slopes.

He texted Will Spalding, the other groomsman from the wedding, whose girlfriend, Penny, was friends with Lindsey, asking if he knew how to get in touch with Lindsey.

He put his head on the steering wheel, feeling like a complete and utter fool.

This was nuts.

Will texted back that he'd ask Penny. A few seconds later he texted a phone number and the word *why*.

Yeah, Shaw, why do you need her number? he asked himself.

He texted that he wanted to talk to Lindsey about the event they were working on at the lodge and wished Will and Penny safe travels as they headed home later in the day.

He was still sitting in his rented SUV, trying to figure out which of the many slopes she'd been taking a run on this morning, when he caught a glimpse of her walking from her car to the lodge. She was wearing a pair of dark pink ski bibs and a cream-colored puffy jacket. Her Nordic blond hair had been pulled back into a ponytail, her hair held back by a ski band around her head.

She looked for all the world as she always had. As if nothing had changed.

He rubbed the back of his neck, thinking that maybe for her nothing had.

It hadn't occurred to him until that moment that prim-and-proper Lindsey Collins, darling of the Alpine ski community, might have used him to get her rocks off on New Year's Eve. It wasn't the first time he'd been a woman's illicit thrill, but on every other occasion he'd known what he was getting into. And he'd been prepared for it.

He'd thought Lindsey was different. He shut off his SUV, got out and followed her across the parking lot and up to the ski lodge and the après ski café. She sat at one of the tables nestled near the big fireplace and facing the slopes. The expression on her face wasn't peaceful or serene.

She looked angry and lost.

Why was Lindsey upset?

Maybe he'd screwed things up when he'd taken her to his bed last night. Another sin to add to his list where this woman was concerned. He walked over to the bar, ordered two hot chocolates and then went to her table.

He set one down in front of her and took the seat next to her so he, too, could look up at the mountain.

"Carter."

"Lindsey."

She pulled the mug closer to her and wrapped her fingers around it, staring down into the whipped cream on the top like a fortune-teller searching for answers.

"What's this for?"

"I'm not sure." He raked a hand through his hair and sighed. "I think I might need to apologize."

"For what? I know *I* should for walking out. But my head's not in the right place this morning. I might do or say something stupid, so I figured I better clear out until…"

He got it. This he understood. He'd spent most of his life clearing out and searching for answers that he still hadn't found.

"No need. I get that. Let's start over," he said.

"How? Do we pretend we never met at seventeen? Or do we act like last night never happened?"

"None of that. Let's just start the morning over." He reached over and clasped her hand in his. "I'm dying to get up on the slopes. You want to go with me?"

"I… Really? I thought you'd want to take it easy."

"I didn't anger all the resort owners here by taking them on and demanding they let snowboarders on the slopes just to be a douchebag. I did it because when I look at that mountain I see something I wanted to conquer. Besides, it was elitist to try to keep us out."

"I never saw it that way," she admitted, staring down at their entwined fingers. "But then, Alpine skiing is accepted everywhere."

"So want to take on the slopes? We can race for real this time," he said. "Not against the clock but against each other."

She slowly withdrew her hand and took a sip of cocoa. "I can't."

He leaned back in his chair and glanced at her. She wasn't watching him but was staring at the mountains again. "I'll go easy on you."

"It doesn't matter. I can't go down the mountain."

"Why not?"

She shook her head. "You were my bit of fun last night, Carter. We're not friends and I—"

"I don't see that you have any friends here right now. Not trying to be mean, but it's obvious—even to this *bit of fun*—that you need someone." He clenched his jaw, trying to keep his temper in check. "I'd like to think over the years I've at least showed you I'm not a total loser."

"I never think of you that way," she said, turning to face him.

He saw something in her expression that he'd never glimpsed there before. It was something more than fear, and if he had to define it, he'd say it looked a lot like disappointment.

"I'm scared, Carter. I can't go down that damned mountain, because every time I've taken the ski lift up there I freeze. I'm fine showing kids what to do in their lessons, but I can't go down a big slope."

His anger instantly cooled. That wasn't what he'd been expecting. Lindsey was afraid? It didn't jive with the bold, fearless woman he'd always known. She'd been throwing herself down the toughest, fastest runs since she'd been ten, or something. She'd gone over sixty miles per hour routinely, and now she was afraid?

"Okay, fair enough," he said. "But we're going to get you over your fear."

She shook her head and took another slip of her hot chocolate. "I don't think so. You're sweet to suggest it, but let's face it, the only thing we've ever had between us is an adversarial—"

"We have more now. We spent the night in each other's arms."

"That was sex," she reminded him. "You always act like sex is just a physical thing. Nothing emotional there."

"Was it for you?" he asked in a low, deceptively calm voice.

"Wasn't it for you?" she countered.

She gave nothing away. Why was he surprised? This was Lindsey Collins, and she never let him have an inch.

LINDSEY DIDN'T WANT to talk about her fears with Carter. In fact, the only thing she wanted was a distraction. God knew he provided her with that.

"I'm sorry I feel like I'm not myself this morning. That's why I left. I can't explain it very well, not even to myself."

"What can't you explain?" he asked, pinning her with his penetrating blue-gray gaze.

"Last night, until the moment you arrived at my table, I was looking at my future and trying to figure out what my next move would be." She sighed. "Last year at this time I was gearing up for a gold medal and setting my future, you know?"

"I do know. But things changed."

"They did, and I ended up here in the bosom of some good friends and in the valley where I first learned to ski and started my world-champion path. I thought this was the place to press the reset button, but it didn't work out that way. I couldn't handle the slopes… I mean, not even the kiddie ones at first. Even now they still scare me."

She tried to stop talking, but the words were just flowing out of her as though they wouldn't be stopped. She'd needed to share this with someone, and Carter, as unlikely as it seemed, was the one person she was finally able to do it with.

"So the reset didn't work," he said, tracing the rim of his mug with his finger.

An image of him doing that exact same thing to her nipple popped into her head and made her squirm in her chair. Dammit. She never thought of sex this way. But Carter had changed her.

"No, it didn't. I have seen a therapist and he suggested it was because reset means I can go back to where I was and that maybe somewhere in my brain is the thought that I don't want to go back there."

He nodded. "My therapist has often said that, for me, I have to keep moving forward. Once I master a skill, I need to find a new one."

"That's interesting… Does he have a theory why?" Maybe there was a clue in Carter's problems that could lead her to a solution of her own.

"He does, but it's very personal." There was a glimpse of the real man. The one he kept hidden behind a curtain of sexy charm and outrageous dares.

"Sorry," she said quietly. "Didn't mean to pry."

"I brought it up. Just throwing it out as an option."

Resting an elbow on the table, he turned to face her. "I want to help you get back on the slopes. It will be a way for me to make up for any part of your crash."

"I told you that wasn't your fault."

"I know, but I need to do this. Plus, and if you repeat this to *anyone* I'll deny it, but when you ski it's like magic. I love watching you on the slopes, and I'd hate to never see you ski again."

"Why would you deny that?" she asked, touched more than she wanted to be.

"Because I'm a bad-boy snowboarder and I've got a reputation to preserve," he said with a wink.

"Well, far be it from me to ruin that for you," she quipped. But deep down inside the freedom she'd felt last night was starting to fade. It made her wistful and wonder how she was going to achieve what had seemed so possible last night. How could she change her life?

"You won't," he said slyly. "So let's see… How's the knee? Have you taken any runs?"

Lindsey shook her head. She thought of how she sometimes brought her skis here and sat as though she'd just taken a run, even though she clearly hadn't.

Who the heck was she trying to fool?

"My knee is fine. No runs. I mean, I'm teaching the classes, so I am on the bunny slopes with my kids, but that's not really skiing."

"Not for you," he said.

"No, not for me. But why do you care? I mean, really. Not that BS about feeling guilty about my crash— the real story."

He leaned in close and shrugged. "Maybe I sense that's the only way you'll let me see you again."

He was right, but she wasn't about to admit it to him.

"We're on a committee together, Carter. We will have to see each other again."

He took a sip of his hot chocolate. "I expected better—more from you than this."

She held the same high expectation for herself. "I'm sorry. I think the combo of too much to drink, a very sexy encounter and confusion left over from last night are making this morning difficult."

"You think too much," he said softly. "I've had more mornings-after than you. Take it from me, you have to just shake it off."

She didn't want to shake it off. A part of her wanted to be the woman she'd been last night. That bold, self-assured, confident woman she'd been with Carter, the woman who'd believed in herself. Surely that hadn't just been the champagne talking. The seeds of that woman had to be inside her.

She just had to figure out how to sow them.

Carter was offering her something by saying he wanted to see her ski again. He'd always been that devilish rogue who could needle her into doing things she'd otherwise pass on.

"Were you serious about helping me ski again?"

"Yes. Thinking of taking me up on it?" he asked, leaning back and giving her a cocky smile. "I knew you would. Women can't resist me."

That was part of her problem. She didn't want to be one of the masses that had been in Carter's life. She wanted to be important and special. And she couldn't. Not right now, because she hardly knew herself anymore.

CARTER REALIZED THAT Lindsey saw him as a bit of fun. And after all the women he'd played around with over the years, a part of him got that it was payback. But another part, the bit where he'd actually thought she was different than all the lovers he'd been with before, bristled. She was looking at him as if he were a stranger. The kind of man that she didn't know or trust.

"What do you say, gorgeous? Want to give it a shot?"

"I do. I'm just not sure that I should be committing to doing anything more with you because you're a bad influence."

He looked at her, amused despite himself by her adorably earnest expression. "How do you figure?"

"Kissing dares. Sex twice in one night… Skiing again."

He noted that she'd started with the light stuff and ended with what was really worrying her. "I'm not going to push you down the slope, Linds. I just want a chance to help you remember what you loved so much about the sport."

She cocked her head to one side, her blond ponytail swinging behind her head, and he remembered the feel of her silky-smooth hair against his body. His blood heated, and he realized that he was working so hard to find a reason to stay in her good graces because he wanted her back in his bed.

He hadn't been finished with her when she'd walked away, and now he had to do whatever was necessary to get her back.

"What do you know about my love of the sport?"

"Only that if I fell and couldn't snowboard for six months, I'd be devastated. And though I'm retiring from amateur competition, I know I still want to be on the board. I can't define myself without it."

She gave him a hard stare. "I hate that you actually get me."

He laughed, but inside a part of him was hurt by that. "Why?"

"You're not a serious person. You think dares and games are the way to get what you want—"

"It's worked for me in the past, hasn't it?"

"You have a point." She sighed. "Maybe this *is* what I need. So what do you recommend?"

"You have to get to the root of your fear."

"How do you know that?" she asked. "Do you have something you're afraid of?"

Of course he did, he thought. But he liked the fact that she saw only the confidence he'd worked so hard at projecting. If she saw him as the man he wanted to be, he was good with that. He wasn't about to start confessing to things that he couldn't do and the secrets he protected.

"Just being walked out on by women like you, gorgeous," he said smoothly.

She nibbled on her lower lip, and he remembered how her mouth had felt under his the night before. He had thought he'd had enough time to exorcise the lust demons that had been plaguing him for years, but realized now he hadn't come close.

Would he ever be able to sate his thirst for Lindsey?

He'd sort of believed that her elusiveness was all that kept him still wanting her. It had been a while, and each time they were apart he'd try to forget her. Those big brown eyes and the pretty blond hair.

The media had dubbed her the Ice Queen for her cool persona before each of her runs. Other skiers smiled and joked, but Lindsey had held herself aloof and had come down the mountain as though she owned it. Now he realized that he had wanted to be the man to melt that icy exterior.

He'd done it once, but that wasn't enough.

Why wasn't it enough?

It seemed to him that having waited so long to claim her in his bed, he should be happy, or at least content. But he wasn't.

He wanted something more.

But as was par for him, he had no way to define it and could only say that it involved Lindsey.

"I am sorry again for leaving so abruptly," she said softly. "I wanted to see if I could take a run this morning... Well, that's not entirely true." She fixed her gaze squarely on his. "You scared me, Carter. I've never been the way I was with you last night. I'm not sure I recognize that part of myself."

"Good," he said. "The old you has been hiding. Frozen in some sort of limbo. I'm glad you don't recognize yourself, because that means you are finally thawing."

"Thawing? Wow, I thought I'd proved last night that there is nothing icy about me," she said in a slightly breathless voice.

"You did, but then you retreated behind your wall of ice," he said.

"Fair enough."

"Let's go," he said, standing and holding out his hand to her.

"Where?"

"Trust me?"

She reached for his hand and gave him a forced smile. "No. But I'll follow you anyway."

He'd take what he could get with her. She stood and he led the way to the parking lot and his SUV.

"Where are we going?"

"You'll see." He smiled mysteriously. "I have an idea."

She got into the vehicle without another word, and he drove them away from the lodge to a path he'd found about a week ago when he'd needed to get away from everyone and everything. He parked the SUV on the side of the road and came around to Lindsey's side of the SUV. She had her door open and had hopped out before he got there.

"This is your big idea?"

"Stop with the doubt and follow me."

He led the way to the tree line over the snow-covered ground, and she followed him. Her boots were good and sturdy, as were his, and he kept walking until he found what he was looking for: a small clearing in the copse of trees. Icicles hung from the branches, and in the center was a mound of snow that he suspected some local kids had built.

"This is it?"

"Yup," he said.

"How'd you find it?" she asked, looking at the steep snow mound, which was large enough to slide down. In the middle was a trench big enough for a sled.

"I don't know, but I think it will work perfectly for us."

She walked over to it and then looked back at him. "Thank you."

Seeing her quiet, contemplative expression as she continued to look at the snow mound made it easy for him to believe that he'd done the right thing. But deep inside he knew that helping her ski wasn't what he really wanted.

6

THE STEEP MOUND of snow might look like a bit of fun to anyone else, but to Lindsey it looked huge. As she stood at the base of it, she realized that Carter had found her the ideal place to test her own limits.

"I have a sled in the SUV," he said. "Let me go and get it."

She nodded.

Words were inadequate while fear was tightening her throat, but really her fear had to do with the public way she'd fallen. She knew everyone had seen it, and now when she put on her skis she was always aware of people watching her. In truth, they might not be, but her fear was that they were.

She noticed some foot holes had been dug in the snow and put her boots in, slowly climbing to the top of the mound. When she got to the top, she simply stood there. Her pulse was racing, and she was sweating inside her snow wear even though it was freezing.

She licked her dry lips and tipped her head back to look up at the sky. This height was so small compared to the mountains she'd skied in her career, yet it felt bigger. Felt scarier somehow, and she knew she didn't want Carter to see her this way.

It was one thing to admit she was afraid to ski but something else entirely to actually let him see a glimpse of what that fear looked like. She turned to climb down and saw him standing there, the trees behind him, their limbs heavy with snow. The small sled in one hand and the most serious look she'd ever seen in Carter Shaw's blue-gray eyes.

He knew.

She hated that he was witnessing this moment of horrible weakness.

He didn't say anything, just continued to watch her. Inside her fear a small bubble of rebellion formed. Carter was the last person on earth she wanted to witness this meltdown.

"Great…I'm glad you have that sled. I was going to give it a try without one but thought I'd wait for you."

"You don't have to do this," he told her. "Baby steps are the way forward."

"I have no idea what you are talking about. This little mound is nothing," she said airily. *God, please let me get off this damned mound, and quickly.*

"Okay." He pointed into the distance. "See that drift over there?"

She glanced all the way across the clearing to the large drift that had been reinforced probably by the same people who'd built this mound. That had to be where the sled would stop. It seemed huge. Farther than anything she'd gone down before.

But she knew that was fear talking.

"Great."

"Great?" he repeated. "I know it's not great, gorgeous."

She knew it, too. But she wasn't about to let him once again see her weak and vulnerable. Man, was that what this was all about? Was that why she couldn't ski? Vulnerability?

Whatever it was, she was going to have to sled down this mound to prove a point to herself—and to Carter. She'd expected him to hand her the sled, but this was Carter, so instead he climbed up next to her.

"Not so bad from up here," he said. "Reminds me of the first time I stood at the mouth of the half-pipe."

"Is this really how high it is?"

"Nah, it's a bit higher, but I was strung out on nerves waiting to take my first run. Excited, scared and so full of ideas of how I wanted it to go I couldn't stand it."

Her hands were shaking, and she wove them together to keep Carter from seeing, but he put one of his big hands over hers. Held them for a minute, and she looked up to see his face close to hers. So close she could see the flecks of silver in his blue-gray eyes and notice how thick his eyelashes were.

He had incredible eyes.

She wanted to do something crazy, like kiss him. *If* she kissed him, then passion could sweep them away and she wouldn't have to go down the mound. Hell, she'd strip down naked in the cold with the wind blowing the snow from the tree branches if it meant she didn't have to go down this small mound of snow.

Realizing that made tears burn at the back of her eyes. Dammit. If she couldn't sled down this freakin' mound, how was she ever going to ski again?

"I'm scared," she whispered.

"I know," he whispered back. He lifted his free hand and cupped the side of her face. "But you are the bravest woman I've ever met."

"Liar."

"I wish. I know that no matter what, you will conquer this mound and then get back on the expert slope. I believe that with every fiber of my being."

His eyes burned into hers, and she could feel the sheer force of his will radiate through her.

But how could he have such unwavering faith in her when she was riddled with so many doubts and fears? She appreciated what he was trying to do here, but a part of her—a huge part—wasn't sure it could really come true.

"I—"

"No, don't say anything else. Just sit your sweet ass on this sled and take the run you've been thinking about."

The run she'd been thinking about was down the Wasatch Back Range, but she had to do this to get there. His strength was there all around her. His breath was warm against her cheek. His hands, which held her so solidly, reminded her that he was virile and strong.

She leaned up and pressed her mouth to his. Angled her lips over his and thrust her tongue into his mouth. Surprised, he opened his mouth, and in her mind she pretended she could borrow his courage just by kissing him. She pulled her head back, took the sled from him and sat before she could think anymore about where she was and what she was about to do.

She put her hands in the snow and shoved with all her might. She wanted to close her eyes as she flew down the mound, but kept them open. Wind whipped past her cheeks as she skidded across the flat snow-packed ground into the drift, and she started laughing.

CARTER HAD ALWAYS been a gambling man. Reaching for things and willing to play the risks, but this was the first time he'd gambled on someone else.

He'd felt as if he'd failed miserably as he'd stood at the bottom and saw Lindsey standing up there literally shaking with fear. It was more than fear or pride or even vulnerability. If he'd had to define it, he would have admitted she was lost. He never wanted to be responsible for that look he'd seen on her face again. So, heart hammering in his chest, he'd climbed up there with her, told her he believed in her. And then, just like that, she'd kissed him and thrown herself down that snow mound as though it was the gate to a Super G course. And when her laughter rang out around the clearing, he'd felt justified, and more than a little bit relieved, if he were being honest.

The risk had paid off.

They spent the next hour sliding down the snow mound. Each time he watched her carefully, and he noticed it wasn't getting easier for her, but she had made up her mind that she would do it.

And she did.

He felt like a jumble of nerves. A mess. This wasn't like him. He was the guy who felt nothing. Why did Lindsey change all that?

And he was beginning to believe that his desire for more of her in his bed wasn't the only thing he wanted.

"Thank you for this."

"You're welcome," he said.

She put the sled on the ground next to him. "Your turn."

He didn't want another turn with anything but her. "Will you go with me?"

"Go with you?" she asked. "Are you asking me to date you?"

Not a bad idea, but they were too old to be dating like that. Weren't they?

"Maybe. But for now I want to take a run down with you."

She nodded.

Picking up the sled, he led her back to the mound and then stood behind her as she climbed up. The woman had a first-class ass, and when she got to the top she glanced over her shoulder and caught him staring at her butt.

"I think you just wanted another chance to ogle me."

"No denying that, gorgeous. I do like your body."

"I like yours, too," she confessed. He climbed up after her and set the sled on the top of the mound. He sat on it and anchored himself in place by stomping his boot into the snow.

"Come on," he said.

Lindsey carefully sat in front of him, scooting back until her buttocks were pressed firmly up against him. He wrapped one of his arms around her waist. She smelled of snow and the pine trees that surrounded the clearing.

"Ready?"

She put her hands together over his arm, holding him as she nodded. He lifted his boot from the place where it was anchoring them in the snow and pushed off with one hand. He leaned in close, holding her to him, and then pivoted his body so they slid sideways into the snow. He fell off the sled and pulled her with him, making sure she was on top of him.

She rested her arms on his chest and looked down at him, and for the first time this morning he saw something close to happiness shining in her big brown eyes. She smiled, and he arched his eyebrow at her. "You must be messing with my mojo."

"I must be," she said. "I've never seen you fall."

"I usually don't," he admitted. But he'd wanted her to see what would happen if she did. Wanted her to experience a fall and maybe in some way show her that this time it wouldn't be as bad as it had been before.

He was messed up. He knew it. He was trying to make her see him in a different light, but the truth was he was too flawed to really want her to see the man behind the bluster. He knew that, but at the same time he sort of wanted her to be the one person who knew the real guy under that cocky facade.

"I imagine this is just one of your seduction techniques. The way you get woman to kiss you."

"Nah, it's how I get women to *let* me kiss them," he said, going along with her. He traced the bottom curve of her lip and held her to him with his arm around her waist. The ground was cold, but he didn't feel it through his snow pants. He looked up at the cloudy sky and saw the first snowflakes falling toward them. One of them landed on the end of Lindsey's nose, and he caught it on his finger and brought it to his lips to lick it off.

She leaned down as another flake landed on his lips, and kissed him. The chilled snowflake melted under the heat of her kiss, and he felt the warmth spread from her mouth to every cell of his body. Slowly working over him until he wrapped both arms around her and kissed her as if nothing mattered except the two of them.

As if there wasn't anything else in the universe but him and her and this snowy clearing. Nothing but her lips moving over hers, her hands on his face and her body pressed intimately to his. Nothing except the taste of her happiness and the cold chill that couldn't penetrate the heat they were generating.

Nothing but he and Lindsey and this outdoor world that they'd both called home for so long.

LYING ON TOP of Carter with the snow gently falling around her was the perfect end to this crazy first day of the year. She had been running on empty, she realized, until he'd pushed her to go down the mound. She wasn't perfect. It was silly to think one man would make that big of a change in her, but this was Carter.

The bad boy who'd been teasing and cajoling her since the moment they'd met. But damn, could he kiss.

Lindsey forgot about everything but how soft his lips were under hers. How right his tongue felt as it tangled with hers. And his taste. It was minty but earthy…and she couldn't get enough of it. Of *him*. His hands were moving up and down her back, cupping her butt and pulling her more fully against him.

Despite the cold, his erection was strong and solid between them, awakening an answering ache deep inside her. She wasn't a sexual person, so this desire so quick on the heels of last night was new. She wasn't sure she wanted to be this lusty. Not with Carter. He had already proved to her that he was different, or rather that *she* was different when he was around.

He made everything she felt seem bigger somehow,

but he also called to the parts of her soul she preferred to keep hidden from the world. She pulled her head back and gazed down into those blue-gray eyes of his. There was something almost harsh about his features, and she recognized the look on his face as smoldering desire. Last night had given her a glimpse into how passion changed him from that sort of mischievous badass into a man who knew how to seduce.

"Let's go back to my room," he said, shifting her so he could sit up.

She shook her head.

"Why not? It's not like—"

Lindsey put her finger over his lips, rubbed it back and forth for a second. Then she brought her finger to her own lips and kissed it. She wanted to be able to dismiss him as easily as she always had. But she couldn't. She thought about how awkward she'd felt this morning and how electrified she felt right now. She wanted him. Wanted to feel his muscled body moving against hers and over hers again. Not again. If she had sex with him again she had to be in control.

"You have to stop thinking that you are the boss," she said, lifting her finger from his lips.

"I'm not?"

"No, you're not."

He swept an errant lock of hair off her cheek. "Then you aren't on fire for me? You don't burn when you think of both of us naked in each other's arms?" His words fanned the flames that were already coursing through her. Of course she wanted that. Just wanted it on her terms. "We'll go to my place. When I say."

"When *you* say?" he asked, quirking one eyebrow at her.

"Yes," she said.

He tightened his arms around her, and she felt him shift before he stood with her in his arms. "I don't think so."

He brought his mouth down on hers, and unlike the last time there was no doubt that he was in charge of this kiss. Her body, which felt as though it wasn't hers anymore, stirred to life. She moaned as he angled his head and deepened the kiss. He held her as if she weighed nothing, but she kept her arms locked around his shoulders. Held on to him.

The only solid thing she could find in a world that she was losing her grip on. A world where all she could see was Carter. She couldn't let him mean that much to her. She knew better than that. He was her sexy midnight man. That was all.

She thought being confused about what to do next was a problem, but dealing with this attraction to Carter was turning into something much harder to handle. She wasn't used to lust or the feelings that coursed through her body. Her skin was so sensitive; her breasts felt full, her nipples tight. She throbbed for him. Needed him between her legs, and she didn't care that they were in this clearing exposed to anyone who happened along. She had to have him now.

That wasn't her.

She didn't need Carter Shaw.

She loosened her hold on him. Startled, she felt his release as she sort of slid down his body and stepped back from him. She didn't like the fever that had engulfed her.

He watched her with narrowed eyes, a flush on his cheekbones, his breath rasping in and out of his body rapidly. She put her hand out and took another step backward, stumbling in the snow and falling, and he stood there watching her. He stretched a hand down to help her up.

"Sorry if that got out of hand. My control disappears around you. I've never wanted a woman the way I want you, gorgeous."

He was getting himself back under control. Giving her that rueful smile of his that made her heart soften and her fears sort of melt away. "Me, either. You make me forget everything I thought I knew about you."

"That's because you didn't know me at all."

She was beginning to believe that. But who was the real man? Did she really want to know? Could she handle him now when she was just barely able to limp forward toward finding herself again?

And could she live with herself if she didn't? He had shown her a world and an experience she'd never found with another man. She really wanted to believe that it was better because she'd experienced it with him.

After all, this morning he'd given her back a piece of the winter world she'd used to love so much. While sledding down the slope wasn't nearly as fast as hitting the Super G course on two skis, it felt like a huge step back to her old self.

7

LINDSEY'S CONDO WAS a little embarrassing now that she saw it through Carter's eyes. She'd always lived sparsely mainly because she and one of her parents—usually her mom—had stayed in this sort of temporary housing during her years of training. Once she'd turned eighteen and started to live on her own, she'd sort of just kept it sparse.

But now as she led him into the two-story condo, she realized how plain and boring it might seem. Carter was surely used to more luxurious accommodations. And this entire bring-him-back-to-her-place-for-sex thing seemed to be backfiring.

"Nice place," he said. "I'm a fan of the Nordic open-air interior design, too."

She couldn't tell if he was serious or having fun at her expense. But she let it go. "Want a drink? Maybe something hot?"

"The only hot thing I'm interested in is you."

"Really? I don't feel hot," she said. Unless being a big, fat, hot mess counted, and she was pretty sure it didn't. But for right now she shoved that aside. She wasn't going to be able to get what she wanted from him if she let her doubts and fears plague her. And unlike standing on all that freshly packed snow earlier, this fear was a lot easier to conquer.

She heard the sound of the television next door coming on. The walls in this place weren't exactly thick. "Sorry about that."

"I have lived in apartments before, so I know what it's like. Why'd you choose this place?" he asked, coming into the room and taking off his coat. He sat on the ottoman to remove his boots.

He was getting comfortable and acting normal. It made her realize how out of sync she felt. She took off her coat and picked his up, hanging them both on hooks by her front door. Her father had put them up when her parents had visited over the holidays.

She kicked her boots off and set them under her coat. Carter came over and did the same with his.

"So why do you live here?" he asked again.

"It's close to the lodge. When I was cleared to ski again, I came back here thinking I'd go straight into training. My coach—do you know Peter Martin?"

"I do. Not sure he likes me very much," Carter said with a huge grin.

"Why does that not surprise me?" she replied. "You do tend to annoy a lot of people."

"I know. I like it."

She knew he did. That had been obvious from the first. "Anyway, I got to the top and couldn't ski down, and he suggested that maybe I stay here and teach classes so I'd be on skis every day as a way of getting used to it again. But so far it hasn't worked."

"Yet it did today. You went down a slope—"

"A tiny one. That hardly counts."

He gave her a chiding look. "But you did it. And we crashed—"

"You did that on purpose," she said.

"You're right," he admitted, taking her hand in his and lifting it to his mouth. He kissed her palm and then placed her hand on his chest. "Guilty as charged. But I had enough of waiting to hold you in my arms. I don't think you can appreciate how much I want you."

She thought that maybe she could. She wanted him, as well. With each aching breath she took she wanted to feel his naked body pressed to hers again. She wanted to see if in the cold light of day he'd been as sexy as he'd been the night before.

Had it been the night and the champagne that had made it seem magical? Surely it had. No man could make her feel so alive. A mountain, maybe. Taking a run down a dangerous slope, definitely. But Carter Shaw—surely she was remembering it wrong.

She felt her pulse beating a little more quickly, and her lips felt dry thinking about his mouth pressed to hers. A slow burning heat brushed over her from head to toe, and her clothes felt too restrictive and she wanted… just wanted things that she'd never thought she would.

He watched her with that uncanny gaze of his and she felt as though he could see all the way through her fears and her doubts. Straight to the heart of her, where she questioned everything she'd experienced with him the night before.

"Gorgeous, what am I going to do with you?" he asked.

A tingle of anticipation swept through her, and she guessed that this was her chance to try out all the risqué things she'd always sort of wanted to try but had never had the right guy to do it with. But this was Carter. The live-for-the-moment poster boy and her chance to do all the things she'd always deemed too dangerous.

"Kiss me?"

He smiled and then lifted one of his hands, pulling the ponytail holder from her hair very carefully so he didn't snag even one strand. He ran his fingers through her hair, fanning it out and pulling it forward over her shoulders. Then he tunneled his fingers through it, tipping her head back, and very slowly lowered his head toward hers.

She kept her eyes open this time. This kiss, she wanted to see his emotions, ascertain what he felt and try to figure out if she was doing this right. Because if she'd learned anything from watching Carter over the years, it was that he knew how to roll with the punches. He moved effortlessly through life and didn't get slowed down by emotional entanglements. Something she knew she had to master before she started to like him any more than she did at this moment.

It could be just sex. Sex was healthy and something she'd never denied herself, but any other kind of attachment wasn't. She'd been focused on skiing and being the best in the world. There hadn't been time for a relationship when she'd eaten, drank and even dreamed about her downhill runs. She had to remember that.

But as his lips moved over hers, just rubbing lightly, and he dropped nibbling kisses along the line of her jaw to her ear, all the while whispering hot promises about all the places he wanted to ravish her, she knew she was in very real danger of forgetting.

LINDSEY KEPT HIM on his toes, always dancing just out of his reach, which normally was exactly what he wanted and needed. But today he didn't. Today he wanted to hold the woman who was so brave and strong but didn't see those qualities in herself. Today he wanted a few moments where he didn't feel as if he had to chase her. And now that they were at her condo—her sparse, non-descript home—he had hoped he'd be able to relax.

But this was Lindsey and she surprised him. Never more so then when he held her in his arms. She wanted him. That was obvious from the flush of her skin and how she kept coming back into his arms when normally she would have been running for the hills.

Last night he'd taken it nice and slow; savored each and every delectable inch of her. But he wasn't sure he could take his time right now. He kept feeling that the harder he tried to keep her by his side the more easily she slipped away from him. And it hit him that the reason was that she saw him the way everyone else did.

As the careless playboy who'd taken too many women to his bed. And for once, he was with a woman that he wanted to be different with, and it wasn't going to happen.

He kissed her, and he meant for it to be a sort of sweet extension of everything that had gone on before, but his control slipped and he plunged his tongue deep into her mouth. His hands tangled in her hair as he urged her head back so that he could get even deeper.

He rested one arm on the wall and leaned in over her, surrounding her yet at the same time keeping some small distance between them. He needed to do that or he was going to rip her clothes off and be on her like a man who hadn't had a woman in years. Instead of just a few hours.

Dammit.

He'd never been this close to the edge of his control.

But Lindsey, with her wide-open, chocolate-brown eyes that gazed up him, searching his face for something— almost daring him to try to make this about something other than sex—goaded him on.

It made him struggle to find a balance between what she expected and what he wanted. That was the key. He knew what he wanted and he had to figure out how to walk that fine edge without revealing to her how desperately he desired her. Not just for this afternoon but for...

How long?

He tore his mouth from hers, reaching for the top of her snow bib and sliding the shoulder straps down. Then he pulled the sweater she wore underneath up and over her head. He tossed it to the floor and stepped back to look at her.

She stood there with the bib folded down from her waist with just a simple cream-colored bra covering her. Her skin was soft; he knew that from the night before. And he remembered how much he'd enjoyed caressing her. She stood there staring at him with that intense gaze that made him harden.

Lindsey took a step forward, grabbed the hem of his shirt and pulled him back to her. She went up on her tiptoes to kiss him as she tugged the fabric up over his chest. He felt her fingers on him. Her nails scraping over his nipples and digging into his pectorals.

"Why do I want you?" she asked under her breath as she pulled her head back. "Why you?"

"There was always something between us, Linds. We both knew that."

He unhooked her bra with one hand and pulled the fabric from her torso. Tossed it on the floor and then leaned down to kiss one nipple. He'd barely had time last night to taste them. They were pinkish red and hardened under his lips. He skimmed his hands over her ribs and down to her narrow waist.

Carter spanned it with both of his hands, pulling her from the wall and more firmly toward him. Then he turned so he could lean against the wall. Her hands roamed up and down, bringing every nerve in his body to red alert.

He wanted her now.

But he was trying to…

Why? Why was he taking this slow when he knew that Lindsey was a sixty-miles-per-hour girl? She liked the exhilaration of speeding through life. But he wanted it to take longer. Needed to tease it out for his as much as her pleasure.

This morning had showed him just how fragile his hold on her was, and he knew that every time he took her in his arms it might be his last.

He lifted his head from her tempting body and looked up at her. Her eyes were half-closed and her skin had a pretty rose-colored blush to it. She was lightly skimming her hands over his skin as she chewed her lower lip.

A moment later she pushed her hands into the waistband of his pants and shoved them toward his feet. He stepped out of them. Then she pushed his boxer briefs down, as well. Standing naked in her hallway, Carter realized he was where he wanted to be. She took his erection in her hand and stroked him up and down while he frantically shoved her clothes out of the way. Then, groaning low in his throat, he lifted her into his arms and turned so that her back was braced against the wall as he thrust into her.

He pushed himself all the way inside her and then

rested his head on her shoulder. He took several deep breaths, but her fingers moving up and down his spine and then lower to cup his buttocks urged him on.

"Take me," she said, whispering the words directly into his ear.

He was already there, moving his hips as she lifted her legs and wrapped them around him, forcing him farther inside her. She tipped her head back, her silky blond hair sliding over his shoulders as he plunged in and out of her.

His world narrowed to just her, and he couldn't think beyond the urge to go deeper, to take her so completely that there wouldn't be a Lindsey and Carter when he stopped, but just one being.

He felt his orgasm at the base of his spine and cursed as he tried to slow it or stop it. But it was too late. He was too close to the edge, and she dug her heels into his thighs, arching up against him as he came inside her. Realizing she wasn't there yet, he reached between their bodies, finding her clit and stroking it while he kept moving in and out of her body.

She felt so good. He felt her tighten around him, and she called his name as she came. He sank to the cold, tiled floor, cradling her in his arms as they fought to catch their breaths. He rubbed his hands up and down her back, and she scooted closer to him, resting her head on his shoulder as his blood pounded in his ears.

"Wow," she said.

Wow. Was that good? He had a feeling as quick as he was, he might not have given his best showing, but he was tired and he'd had that feeling all day that he might never have all he wanted from her.

"That good?" he asked gruffly.

"Yeah. I had no idea… My sexual experience isn't as diverse as yours. I mean, mission-style, lights off is my usual thing." He would've laughed if he'd thought that was what she wanted from him. "We've had the lights on every time."

"Yes we have. You make me feel so comfortable in my skin," she murmured. "Other guys seemed to just…"

Jealousy shot through him. The last thing he wanted to talk about were other guys she'd been with. But he was glad she felt comfortable around him. "I'm glad I didn't disappoint you."

"Me, too. So what now? I invited you back here so I wouldn't have to feel awkward and wonder if I should leave, but to be honest, I still feel weird."

He shook his head. Lindsey was never going to react the way he thought she would. She surprised him yet again, but really that was proving to just be her way. "I'll take that hot drink you offered, and then we can figure out what to do—or I can leave." Turning toward her, he slowly searched her face. "What do you want?"

She hesitated, and at that moment he knew she was going to send him on his way. Disappointment churned inside him, but he kept his game face on. "Okay. Let me clean up and then I'll head out."

Lindsey stood. She smelled of sex and regret, he thought. But then she offered him her hand. "Silly boy. I'm not done with you yet."

He took her hand and got to his feet, making sure his body brushed against hers. Felt her shiver, saw her lick her lips. God, was he really willing to be her boy toy? Because that was how this felt.

"A hot bath would be perfect after all that playing,

but my tub is smallish. What do you say to sharing a shower?"

"I say hells to the yeah."

"Good. That's one of the things I meant to put on my resolutions list from last night," she said.

"I actually have it right here," he told her, bending to pick up his pants and pull out the card he'd shoved in there before he'd left his hotel room.

She reached out to take it from him. "I have a lot of blanks."

"So do I," he admitted ruefully. But in his mind he'd already started filling them in.

"Shower first, and then we can fill them in together and order pizza because I'm hungry. Then you can head home. Is that okay?" she asked after a moment.

He nodded. "It's your show, lady."

"It is?" She blew out a breath, biting down on her lush lower lip. "It's not easy to believe that. I'm totally winging it here."

"So am I. This is different for me, too."

She took his resolution card from him and glanced down at it, wrinkling her brow as she read the few words he'd jotted down.

Crap. He wasn't good with words or spelling. He had dyslexia, which was something he didn't share with the world. And something he certainly hoped she hadn't picked up on. He'd brought her list because he wanted to know what she expected from her year.

He should have left his at home.

But there was no point in worrying about that now. He scooped her up in his arms. Taking the stairs two at a time, he paused on the landing. "Which way?"

"Second door on the right," she said. Nodding, he

carried her into her room. This space seemed more like Lindsey—there was a bright floral-patterned comforter and a large stack of pillows at the head of the bed. The walls had been painted a pale blue color that reminded him of the reflection of the snow and sky first thing in the morning. He saw her medals hanging on the wall under a photo of her with the president.

Carter set her on her feet, and she put the cards on her dark-finished, solid-oak dresser as she led the way to her bathroom. She bent to get some towels from the cabinet, and he realized that there was something about Lindsey that would always leave him wanting more. That being here with her now wasn't doing anything but making him crave her more intensely.

He wondered if he'd ever get his fill of her, but then she turned, held her hand out to him, and he stopped thinking and questioning. At least for now, he was exactly where he needed to be.

8

IT'S A BAD IDEA. She knew she had to say it as soon as they were done eating the pizza they'd ordered. They weren't going to be a couple or start dating. She was a mess and he had to know it.

But she liked him. He was fun and he made her feel as though she was a fun person, too. Except that she was also acutely aware that she wasn't really the woman she acted like around him.

She'd had more sex in the past twenty-four hours than she'd had in the previous ten years; which was both great and confusing. She couldn't keep the compartments she needed Carter to stay in straight in her mind.

"Stay or hit?" he asked.

They were playing poker…well, blackjack or twenty-one, at her kitchen table. She wore her flannel pajamas and Carter had on just his boxer briefs. It felt intimate and cozy and would be if she'd just let it be. But she couldn't.

She glanced at her cards, trying to recall the rule that Carter had shared with her for taking cards. She had an eight and a three. She needed twenty-one and had eleven. Seemed pretty safe for a hit.

"Hit."

He turned a card up in front of her. *Ace.*

"Damn."

He laughed. "I'm guessing you want to stay?"

She shook her head. Had she given the game away? She hated to lose, so she needed to pay better attention, but the truth was Carter was a distraction with his naked chest and tattoos sitting across from her. The light from the kitchen shone down on him, his face hidden by the shadows cast on him.

"No," she said. No guts, no glory had always been her motto. "Hit."

He gave her another card. It was a seven. A nice, safe little seven card that kept her from going over twenty-one.

"Stay."

"Think you can beat me?"

He had a face card showing, so chances were he might have a twenty but... What? She'd just said no guts... "You bet I do."

He took a card and got another face card.

"Ooh, that's twenty. Did you bust?" she asked.

He flipped up his card to reveal a two. "Why, yes, I did, gorgeous. That means you win."

"That's right, I win," she said, smiling. This was good. Competing against Carter reminded her of all the things that were usually between them.

"Now you have to tell me the one habit you are hoping to break this year," she said. They'd been playing loser-tells-all for their resolutions.

"Fair enough, but I'm going to ask you about sexual positions. Sure you don't want to know about them?"

"I don't have to win a game to get you to tell me about them," she said. "Now, what habit is it that you want to quit?"

He scratched his chin. "I think I'd like to quit… Wait—does it have to be a vice?"

"Not at all. You get to choose."

"Well, then, I will quit answering these questions," he said insolently.

She narrowed her eyes at him. "That's *already* your habit. And we both agreed to the terms. You have to answer." He leaned back in the chair so his expression was visible now. She looked over at him, trying to figure out what was going on behind his handsome face. He was too sexy for his own good. It would have been better if he'd been average looking with that personality of his. He was used to charming anyone—man or woman—into doing whatever he wanted. She was determined to be different.

Hell, that had been her attitude from the beginning. Had she been attracted to him all this time?

"Well, if you must know…" he said. "I'm going to give up pulling all-nighters. I think I'm past the point where I can keep drifting through life."

She almost laughed, but she knew he was being sincere. He was one of the top athletes in winter sports and he thought he was drifting through life. She kind of got it because that was how she felt now that skiing had been taken from her.

"So what does a serious Carter Shaw look like?" she asked.

"Ah, that, gorgeous, is a second question, and I'm

afraid you've only earned one," he said with that half grin of his that she found way too irresistible. "Besides, that's not on the resolutions list. I might answer it if you win again."

"So deal," she said. Now that she was getting the hang of the game and she'd won, she was ready to keep winning. It was a sort of safe way for her to find out more about Carter. Learn all the intimate details about him while keeping her own secrets safe.

"Don't forget there is a little thing called beginners luck," he warned as he dealt her two cards.

"I've never relied on luck. Just skill and grit. Something that I guess a drifter like you wouldn't understand."

"Touché."

Her cards weren't so good this time. A five and a nine. Fourteen. It almost felt as if she should stay, but she wanted to win again.

Carter had a three showing.

"Hit me."

He flipped a card up in front of her. A three. Not what she'd been hoping for, but she smiled as if it was the only thing standing between her and twenty-one and gestured that she'd stay.

"That good, eh?"

She shrugged. "Like I said…no luck needed here."

It was funny, but she'd forgotten how often she'd had to use her press face with people in the real world to mask what she was really feeling. And now she was doing it playing cards. She'd never tell him, but Carter was giving her back little pieces of herself she hadn't even realized she'd lost when she'd stopped skiing.

Things such as bluffing, which didn't seem to have much in common with her skiing life but actually did.

He took a card and got a nine. "I'll stay. What have you got, gorgeous?"

She flipped up her cards. "Seventeen."

"Aw, that might be enough to beat me if I didn't have…"

He flipped his card over. An eight.

An eight!

"Looks like I win."

"Looks like you do," she agreed. "What are you going to ask me?"

He leaned forward, that blue-gray gaze of his intense—so intense she couldn't look away—as he took her hand in his. "Will you give me a shot, or is this just a one-night stand?"

HE HADN'T MEANT to ask her that, but now that he had, he knew that was exactly the only thing he wanted an answer for. Today had been one of the best of his life. But there was a part of him that realized she had pegged him into the casual category and he knew he wanted more.

He had to know what he was up against. Just like each time he stood at the lip of the half-pipe and took a breath before taking his run. Each half-pipe was different. Each run unique. And he prepared for the different mountains and the different events as if he'd never taken a run at it before.

Lindsey was like an unfamiliar run. This was his first time with a woman who mattered. *She* mattered. The words echoed around in his brain as he sat at the table trying to be cool. Or as cool as a guy could be wearing just his underwear while playing cards.

It had felt right until this moment when he'd laid everything out in front of her. He saw in her eyes the moment she thought she'd come up with an answer. She tipped her head to the side and gave him that smile he'd seen on her face in photographs a million times.

"What kind of shot?" she asked coyly.

"One where you don't wear a fake smile," he said.

Sure, he loved games, but not with her. Or at least not with her at this moment.

"I honestly don't know what to say." She released a breath. "I think it's a bad idea to take this any further. Because like I already told you when I left your hotel room this morning, I'm dealing with some stuff. It's not fair to get involved with anyone at this moment."

He nodded and leaned back in his chair. "Fair enough." He wanted to argue but he knew that he wasn't going to change her mind. Not right now anyway.

"That's it? I was expecting an argument or some passionate plea to give you a shot," she said.

"Do I look like I have to beg a woman to be with me?" he asked. But that was pride making him stupid. He shouldn't have said it and knew it the moment the words had left his mouth.

"No, you look like a guy who has too many women saying yes… I think I've had enough of games for today. Why don't we call it a night?"

Damn. He should say something—apologize—but she'd slammed him hard in the ego and he wasn't ready to let her know that. Doubted he ever truly would be.

"Good idea," he said.

Carter left her kitchen and went to the hallway, where his clothes sat in a pile, and got dressed. He'd pushed too hard, he knew it, but could see no way to back out of this without admitting he was an ass.

He heard her in the hallway and looked up to see her hovering in the doorway. The expression on her face was unreadable, and he wondered if there was anything he could say. He wished he was better at interacting with people, would give up his ability to do a 360 for the chance to make this right.

"I— Thank you, for today," she said quietly. "Thanks for the fun in the snow and…everything else. I needed it. You've helped me kick off this year with a great start."

She was classy. He had to admit even when showing him the door, she did it in such a way that he almost didn't mind. He had sensed from the first moment they'd met that there was something different about her and now he knew what it was.

She had a kind, beautiful heart.

Lindsey had that innate goodness that he'd never been able to find. Even when he wanted to be nice, it usually came off as self-serving. He'd tried, but around her it was easy to see that he would continue to fail.

"What can I say? It's all a part of the Carter Shaw package." He bent to tie his boots, and then straightened to face her.

"Don't do that," she said.

"Do what?"

"Make it sound like you don't feel things like I do." Their gazes met and held, and he could see a depth of emotion glimmering in her beautiful brown eyes.

"What makes you believe that I could?"

"I spent the day with you, Carter. I saw a side of you that few people ever do, and I'm so glad I did." She reached up and gently squeezed his biceps. "I like you."

But she was still kicking him out. "Gosh, thanks."

"Stop it. You know what I mean. I had no idea that behind that big braggart and awesome talent was a man who could see past his own ego and help me try to conquer my fears. I really can't thank you enough."

His jaw flexed and he swallowed hard. That was nothing. He hated that he might be even the tiniest bit responsible for her not skiing anymore, and he didn't want to think of the winter sports without her. For him the two things were inexorably tied together. So even his unselfish move of trying to get her back on skis had turned out to be for him.

"You're welcome," he said at last, because he really didn't know what else to say. There was a part of him that knew if he was an eloquent man, maybe more like his old man, he'd come up with just the right sentiment to express.

But he wasn't that guy.

He was a tattooed snowboarder who'd been searching all his life for the next big thrill. The next adrenaline-fueled high he could find. He'd never have guessed that he'd find it in this cool Nordic blond, Alpine Super G skier who always seemed to look right through him.

"Goodbye," he said.

He turned, opened the door and forced himself to walk away without looking back. But he wanted to see if she watched him as he left. Wanted to know if he'd had an impact on her the way she had him. But was afraid to see the truth: that he might need her more than she wanted him.

LINDSEY STEPPED INTO the boardroom at the Lars Usten lodge with more than a little trepidation. It had been two weeks since she'd sent Carter away, and she wasn't sure if he'd be at this meeting or not. She'd been back to that little snow mound three more times.

The first time she hadn't been able to go down the hill on her sled. The second time she'd gotten mad, climbed to the top and stood there shaking until she'd forced herself to slide down. It had been hard, but she'd forced herself to do it three more times before going home, and then yesterday she'd gone and just did it. The fear was still there, but she was finding her strength again.

This weekend she hoped to get back on her skis and actually go down one of the easier runs in the Wasatch Range. But today she had to get through a corporate meeting.

She just didn't like having to dress up and sit in a stuffy boardroom. The lodge itself was rustic and homey. First-class luxury. She loved the large patios that overlooked the picturesque mountain vistas and the pristine ski trails.

"You're one of the first to arrive," Elizabeth Anders said, coming over to give her a hug. "I'm glad. I have missed our breakfasts and was hoping you'd have time for a coffee before we get started."

Her friend was the general manager of the lodge and had recently—as in on New Year's Eve—married her best friend, Bradley. Lindsey had been one of the bridesmaids at the ceremony.

"I didn't know exactly when you were getting back from your honeymoon today," Lindsey said. "I've missed our breakfasts, too. Too much time alone with myself and my thoughts."

"Like what?" Elizabeth asked as she led the way down the hall to where a coffee service was set up.

"Nothing. Just some crazy decisions I made on New Year's Eve," she said as she made herself a cup of coffee. No way was she going to elaborate on what had gone down with Carter. But it was nice to have her friend back, so maybe for a little while she didn't have to keep thinking about it.

"How was your honeymoon?"

"Fab. The Lars Usten Resort in the Caribbean was really nice. And it was a change of pace to be a guest and not have to always be watching for things that might go wrong."

Lindsey laughed. Elizabeth looked polished from head to toe, like someone who had everything all together. Even when she was going through the ups and downs of falling in love with Bradley she'd still done it with panache.

Something that Lindsey never felt she had.

"That's great."

"Are you okay?" Elizabeth asked, her brow in concern. "You don't seem yourself today."

Lindsey nodded. "Just nervous about this meeting. I know what the event is supposed to be but I've never been on a committee before."

"You'll do fine. It's nothing like skiing sixty miles per hour."

Lindsey gave Elizabeth the smile she was sure her friend was looking for. But she knew that skiing wasn't easy, and this meeting wouldn't be, either. Of course, she could contribute and she'd do whatever she had to to make the charity ski event a success.

The event had been proposed by Carter and had taken a lot of the resort owners in the area by surprise. The last time he had proposed something it had been to allow snowboarders on the runs in the valley; something that had gone against the resort owners' policies. He'd won them over, and now skiers and snowboarders were welcome on the mountain, but he hadn't exactly endeared himself to the owners with that move.

So the charity event, which would bring world-class athletes and young kids interested in winter sports together, had initially caught the higher-ups off guard. Lindsey smiled to herself at the thought of how shocked the owners had been to see their old nemesis in a different light.

Not unlike the way she was. Carter had changed, and he'd sort of changed her. She missed having him around, but wouldn't admit it to herself or to anyone else. She figured if she had a few restless nights plagued with dreams of making love on her kitchen table with Carter, that was the price she had to pay for peace of mind.

"Hello, ladies," he said, walking up to her and Elizabeth. Seeming to appear from out of nowhere.

She took a sip of her coffee and burned her tongue. He looked good. Polished in that roguish way of his. Elizabeth and he were chatting, but all she could do was watch him and acknowledge to herself that her dream-induced fantasies fell far short of the real man. She missed him.

No denying that.

"Well, Linds, how's the skiing going?" he asked after Elizabeth excused herself to greet some of the other committee members.

"Great," she said. No use telling him she still hadn't made it up the mountain. That was her personal struggle. "How long are you here for?"

"For the next six months."

Her eyes widened. "What? Why that long?"

"This charity event is my number one priority right now," he said. "And I told you I was going to get you back on skis. I can't do that from California, now, can I?"

"I think you've done enough. Feel free to go back to Cali."

He leaned in close to her and the spicy scent of his aftershave wrapped around her, reminding her of how strong the scent had been when she'd rested her head on his shoulder after making love.

"I promise you I haven't done nearly enough."

9

CARTER SAT ACROSS from Lindsey in the meeting. He was excited for the event and when he'd originally come up with the idea had known it was going to be a hard sell. Truth was, he'd never really played up to the resort owners in Park City, Utah, and the surrounding valley. They had sort of always looked down on snowboarders, but he wasn't Houston Shaw's son for nothing, and had learned from his father that turning adversaries into business partners made for some interesting and profitable ventures.

But this wasn't about profit. This was about bringing snowboarding and skiing to kids who couldn't afford it otherwise. Giving them the chance to have what he'd always had. To be honest, he hadn't realized how much of a financial struggle competing at the world-class level could be, since he'd had the benefit of his father's money.

Lindsey understood that. She spoke eloquently on the fact that it wasn't just inner-city kids or those at the lowest economic level who needed help, but also middle-class families who were getting by—as her family had when her talent had been spotted.

"I think we're all on board now," Lars Usten, the namesake and owner of the resort, said. "We just need to figure out what the event will look like."

"I see it as a three- or four-day event," Carter told them. "Starting on a Thursday with events for the kids who've maybe signed up through our program to have lessons."

"What program?" Elizabeth asked. "Is this something new to the agenda?"

"Yes," Carter said. He passed around some folders that outlined his idea. "Since we're not doing the event until the fall, I propose we start getting local kids involved in training sessions now. I'd like to see each of your resorts offer up your facilities, and maybe we can have teams to compete against each other."

Everyone had opened the folder and was skimming the contents. He had done a lot of work.

"Bradley Hunt of FreshSno is donating the gear for the kids, and Thunderbolt, my energy drink sponsor, will give the kids the clothing they need," he said finally. "Ski pants, jackets and a T-shirt. All I really need now is your resorts and time on the slopes."

"That's great, but who's going to teach the kids? We all have full-time jobs," Lindsey reminded him. "Not everyone is a man of leisure like you."

"Well, I'm going to teach snowboarding. It's what I'm good at and, as you've pointed out, I do have the time. I'm sure there must be a few former world champs who wouldn't mind teaching the next generation."

"I didn't say I minded," Lindsey said, bristling at his insinuation. "Of course I'll do it on my days off. These will just have to be needs based and when I'm not teaching the kids from the resort."

"Good. So now we've got Alpine skiing and snow-boarding," Carter replied.

"I've got an idea," Bradley said. "Watching you two square off... What if we put together two teams, captained by each of you, to raise funds? Anyone who follows winter sports knows that you are adversaries—the Ice Queen versus the Bad Boy." He smiled broadly. "It's classic and fun. We can have people from the committee and other resort staff members on the teams as well as the kids. What do you think?"

Carter liked it. It was an innovative idea and would give him a chance to spend more time with Lindsey. A legitimate reason that she wouldn't be able to back out of. "Sure. I think it's got some merit. Plus, it's for charity. I want to see it be a success."

Lindsey glared at him from across the table. He wasn't sure what it was he was doing today, but he seemed to be getting on her nerves. *Perfect.* He wanted her to be aware of him and to be bothered by him. It seemed only fair, since she was bothering him.

He was here because of a cause that was dear to him. He'd seen a lot of talented kids over his years in the sport that'd had to quit because they couldn't afford gear. That wasn't right.

But then, as he stared back at Lindsey, a telltale smirk suddenly tugged at his lips. Okay, if he was being *totally* honest, his reasons for being here weren't entirely altruistic. It was also because he'd wanted to see her again and this was the only way he'd been able to do it. She'd shut him out. He'd thought about calling, but he wasn't going to keep chasing her. At least not in an obvious way.

"I want it to be a success, too. I'd be happy to captain a team," Lindsey said, her fake smile firmly in place.

"Okay, then. How are we going to choose teams?" Elizabeth asked. "We have two representatives from all the resorts and other participants here, so we could do it that way. One from each?"

There was some discussion around the table of the different skills, but soon the teams were established and Carter thought he'd made out pretty well. Most of the owners and executives from the resorts were passionate skiers.

"We'll need to come up with events. And they should be pretty standard but not risky," Lindsey said.

"It should be fun, too. We want to bring new people to the sport and make it something the kids will want to do. In fact, maybe we can use our teams as mentors," Carter suggested.

"That's a great idea," Lars said. "I'll be in charge of the events for our competition. I think we should hold it in February to kick off our announcement for the fall event. Use it to encourage kids to sign up."

There was agreement around the table. Lars asked each of them to jot down one or two ideas for events for the kickoff to be held in February. A meeting was set for the following week and everyone left the boardroom.

Carter gathered his papers and followed Lindsey down the hall and out onto the patio that led to the ski rental and lesson building.

"Wait up."

"Sure," she said, whirling around to face him. "Think of something else you wanted to challenge me on?"

"Not at all. I told you I wasn't done with you," he warned.

"I know that. I'm not done with you now, either."

She wasn't really angry with him. On the contrary,

he could see worry and maybe a little bit of fear on her face. She couldn't ski, and she'd just been put in charge of a ski team for a major public event.

Crap.

SHE HADN'T MEANT to talk to Carter. She'd meant to exit the lodge, get into her ski clothing and then... What? She had no real idea. Obviously she couldn't lead a team down the slopes in February considering that just sledding down a little snow mound took all of her courage.

But she had to. Everything had changed thanks to this guy and his damned argumentative streak. She had a hunch that he'd originally started sparring with her in front of everyone as a sort of payback for the way she'd kicked him out of her place on New Year's Day, and frankly, she hadn't blamed him.

But this... She put her arm around her waist.

"Okay, this is serious. I already offered to help you and I'm not going to let this go," he said.

"Carter, thanks, but you can't make that fear I feel when I strap on a pair of skis go away. I mean, you seem to be able to charm anyone into doing anything, but this is something I don't think even you can simply force under your control."

She dropped her arm as she realized how defensive that might look to him. Then she spun on her heel and started walking again. As she moved across the resort grounds, she paused to look around her. It was the kind of day she used to love. The snow was thick, perfect for a fresh run, and the sky looked clear and endless. This was her favorite sort of winter.

"I know that," he said, quickly catching up with

her. "I'm just saying every time I dare you to do something—"

"It backfires," she retorted. The bet on a kiss that had started all of this hadn't spurred her on to greater skiing glory. Or had it? She'd kept her head down and trained harder to prove he didn't bother her. That his flirting couldn't shake her. Maybe that was what she needed to do now. Put her head down and pretend he couldn't affect her.

"I've got this."

"You know," he said, "it wouldn't hurt you to admit that you can't do it all on your own."

"I don't need an entourage to remind me— What is it exactly that they do for you?" she asked sweetly.

"Nothing. They are friends, not an entourage. Something that seems foreign to you." He reached out and gripped her arm. "You have people who care for you, but you are always so afraid to let them in."

"Let *you* in," she said, jerking away. "That's what you really mean."

"True. Why is that?"

She stopped walking and looked over at him. He had put on a pair of sunglasses so she couldn't see his eyes. "You scare me. You make me confused. I don't really like it."

"I don't like it, either, but we are going to have to work together."

"Why?" she asked.

"I'm the only person who knows you haven't skied since your surgery, aren't I?"

She nodded. When she got home she was taking that damned resolutions list off the fridge and adding "no drinking champagne" to it. Maybe if she hadn't been drinking she wouldn't have found him as attractive and confessed all sorts of things she should have kept to herself.

"Carter, please. Just let this go. I'll figure it out and no one will have to know anything," she said.

"I can't."

She sighed in frustration. "Why not?"

"Because you made me your New Year's resolution and I'm determined to give you a year you won't forget."

"I was drunk when I said that," she said. But despite her annoyance with him, his words made her feel warm like the sunshine on her face. There was more to Carter Shaw than she wanted to admit. Mainly because if she didn't keep him at arm's length she might do something foolish, like fall for him.

And it was foolish. Though she hadn't seen him in person for the past two weeks, she'd seen him online on the gossip websites with a bevy of women at the Thunderbolt Energy Drink Extreme Winter Games as he'd promoted his upcoming professional debut in California. She knew that he was a player.

She had to seem like a novelty to him. And while she got that to him she was different, a challenge of sorts, how long would it take for that to wear off and for him to move on? She wasn't being down on herself. She had plenty to offer a man, but not one like Carter. His expectations were based on a model of woman and a lifestyle that made hers seem boring.

"You weren't drunk. If you want to pretend you were, then fine," he said tersely. "I don't know why I keep chasing after you."

She didn't know, either, and she wasn't foolish enough

to guess. "Thank you. I guess I'll see you next week at
our meeting."

"Yes, you will."

She walked away and admitted to herself that she was
disappointed he'd let her go. She'd hoped that maybe
he'd follow her. But she knew she'd have shut him down
if he had.

She got changed in the locker room and, as usual, putting on her ski clothes brought out that little bit of sad-
ness and fear. But she had a class to teach, and letting
down her students wasn't something she'd do.

Her first lesson went well, and instead of just holding
her skis, this time she put them on and skied around a
little bit while the kids met their parents for lunch. She
was going to try to take a run after lunch.

The clock was ticking and she wasn't about to let
anyone else know her secret. It was time she conquered
that fear and moved on. Then maybe she could figure
out what to do about her attraction to Carter.

10

LINDSEY SURVEYED HER TEAM. She had Bradley Hunt, Lars Usten, Stan Poirier from Thunderbolt and two other executives from other resorts in the area. She had been practicing sledding every day on her little snow mound, as well as getting used to standing at the top of a slope and going down.

But she was nowhere near as ready to take on a downhill race as she'd need to be if her team was going to win. Beating Carter was important to her. She needed it. He had seen her flustered and flawed and she wanted to wow him.

"Okay, team, welcome to our first practice. I thought we'd talk a little about the skills each of you has and then decide how to proceed."

"I'll go first," Lars said. The former world champion still skied every day, and he was in pretty good shape despite a health scare back in November. "I'm probably the biggest liability on the team since my heart attack at Thanksgiving, but I want you all to know I've been skiing every day and my runs are getting faster and smoother."

"I don't think anyone doubted you, Lars," she reassured him. "I've always been in awe of your control while you're on skis."

"Thank you, Lindsey. Coming from you, that's a compliment I'll treasure," he said with a smile.

He reminded her of her grandfather in a lot of ways. Except hers didn't really like to ski. Lars was the kind of grandfather she would like to have.

"I'm more into sponsoring crazy athletes than actually doing the crazy stuff myself."

"Sponsoring athletes is what you are good at," Lindsey said.

"I've already sent an email to the committee agreeing to that." Bradley grinned. "Oh, and by the way, I have a feeling my wife is going to want to compete against me."

Lindsey rolled her eyes. "That would hardly be fair, since you just started skiing."

"I know. I think that's why she keen on it," Bradley said with a laugh.

Clearing his throat, Stan added, "My wife, Georgina, is better than I am. She might want to go against someone like you, Lars."

"This is all good to get out in the open, but let's face it, we have to train to do our best times," Lindsey informed the group. "Now, I suspect that Carter is going to want to go down on his snowboard, and I think the committee has agreed to let him. Does anyone else snowboard?" Tim and Paul raised their hands. She talked to them briefly, but frankly she didn't snowboard so couldn't really "coach" them.

Bradley left to take a call, and during the hour-long practice that followed, Lindsey spent most of her time writing down the times of the others and waiting for them to finish with various business calls. It was obvious this wasn't going to be like training for an international event.

In addition to practicing, they'd sell tickets to the event, and each member of the team was to fund-raise. The group was breaking up when Bradley returned. Whistling under his breath, he was obviously in a good mood. Lindsey wished she felt the same. She was upset with herself that she hadn't taken a run. Deep down she wasn't even sure she could do it, but she knew she was going to have to. Either that or admit to everyone in this microcosm that she wasn't the skier she used to be.

"Hey, I just got off the phone with a college buddy of mine who is an orthopedic surgeon for the military," Bradley announced. "He mentioned that some of the vets who've been wounded overseas and lost limbs have a winter sports team." He paused. "I was wondering what your thoughts were about getting them involved. He gave me the number of their team captain."

"I love this idea," Lindsey said.

Everyone else agreed, too, so Bradley sent a group email to the other committee members.

"Once we get everyone's acceptance, maybe you could liaise with him, Lindsey?" Lars asked. "I think we've all proved you can take the executive out of his office but you can't make him stop working."

She laughed, as she was sure he'd intended. "No problem. I have time between classes to make a few calls."

"Perfect. Let's meet back here next week, and if anyone needs any pointers or one-on-one coaching, I'm available."

The group left, and she walked to her office at the back of the ski rental office aware of the fact that she was a total fraud. She wondered how she was going to get over this. How was she going to make herself ski when it was the last thing she thought she could do?

Right now, sitting in her office, looking up at the mountain, she felt dread and fear. She should just confess and stop trying to be something she used to be.

"Knock, knock," Carter said from the doorway. "Got a minute?"

Definitely. Her breath hitched as their eyes met and held. She'd rather spar with him than dwell on her own inadequacies. "Sure. Come to tell me that your team isn't up to snuff? Mine is great."

"Ha. Mine is pretty good, too. Elizabeth can really ski, and I was surprised that Georgina could, as well. Don't tell either of them. It's just that they never talked about skiing."

"I know what you mean. I've got two snowboarders and I'm not really sure how to handle them. But they are pretty good. Not you good, of course, but still, they've got some skills."

"It's hard to be as good as me," he said with that big sexy grin of his.

A shiver of awareness skittered down her spine as she gazed into his blue-gray eyes. It had been days since she'd been alone with him, and instead it felt like years. Everything about him turned her on. His disheveled hair, his baggy snowboarding pants, the spicy scent of his aftershave. New Year's Eve had whetted her appetite, and she wanted more of Carter Shaw. And right now flirting and playing with him felt safe.

CARTER FOUND IT harder and harder to keep up the casual pretense he'd cultivated around Lindsey. He missed her.

He physically ached for her and wanted to do whatever he could to get her back into his bed, but she was setting the limits, and right now that meant taking it slow.

Sitting in the small office and smiling when what he really wanted to do was to pull her into his arms, run his fingers through her long, silky blond hair and kiss her until she was panting. But that wasn't going to happen. He was pursuing her but didn't want her to know it. He needed to keep up appearances. And that was exactly what he intended to do.

"It is hard to be as big as your ego," she said glibly. "I wish I had a tenth of it."

"What do you need it for?"

"I have to ski at our event in the middle of February, Carter. I haven't done anything but slide down a mound of snow since I crashed last year in Sochi. What am I going to do?" she asked.

Looking as though she had the weight of the world on her shoulders, she walked around her desk and sat on the edge of it, right in front of him. He saw a hint of vulnerability in her eyes. She needed him. It felt good. Stroked his ego. And she'd probably never let him live it down if he let her know.

"Take a run with me."

"I don't even know if I can. You saw me on the snow pile. I was shaking like an idiot up there. If I was on skis—"

"I've got an idea," he said.

"I doubt it would work."

"My last one did," he said, bragging just a little, but also making a challenge out of it. He knew how she was. She'd rise to the challenge.

Lindsey sighed impatiently. "Fine. What's your idea?"

"Just a ride down the mountain in a toboggan."

"I don't know."

"I'll be with you," he said gently. "You know, like I was at the snow mound."

She watched him with wary eyes, and he ached that she had lost her faith in herself. He vowed he'd do whatever he had to do to help her get it back.

"Would we go here at the lodge?" she asked.

"Yes. We could even say we are checking it out for an event for our nonskiers. I've got two of them."

"I didn't get one. Maybe we can swap one of my snowboarders for your nonskier. It's always weird to me when people live and work this near the Wasatch Range and they don't ski."

"Me, too," he admitted. "I can see it in Cali because there are so many other sports that people can do, but here? It's pretty much ski or snowboard. Or, at the very least, ice skate. Speaking of which…you ever try that?"

She shook her head. "I'm not that good at it. Plus, my coach used to like me to focus on my sport."

"Good idea. My coach said something similar but I did it anyway."

"Rebel."

"You know it," he said.

Lindsey bit her lip, then turned to stare out the window before finally looking back over at him. "I wish I had your courage."

"You do have it. But in your own way. You are a rebel when you need to be. I've seen you when you pass through the gates for the downhill. You look very fierce."

He had never mentioned it, but the first time he'd noticed Lindsey was after her run. She'd broken the world-record time. He'd been so turned on by her he hadn't known what to do. She hadn't been his kind of woman, but then suddenly his body had been, like, hell yeah, she is.

"Thank you, Carter. You know, for an egomaniac, you say some really nice things," she said, tipping her head to the side to study him.

"I'm not as ego driven as you think I am."

"Really? You're not going to convince me." She checked her watch. "But I can probably take off in about an hour if you want to try the tobogganing idea."

"Great." He was shameless where she was concerned, using her love of skiing and her need to be back on her skis as a way to keep him by her side. He wondered if she would still be talking to him after their night together if it wasn't for the fact that she couldn't get back on her skis.

It was humbling, and he didn't like the way it made him feel, so he treated those feelings the way he usually did. He shoved them so far down he could pretend they didn't exist.

"I'll go to the concierge and make sure we can get on there and then come back in an hour," he said. It would probably be a good idea to give her some space so she could miss him.

"Okay. Thanks, Carter," she said.

"For?"

"Just being a friend."

Friend. Ugh. He wasn't about to let her relegate him there. Glancing over his shoulder to make sure no one was nearby, he closed the gap between them and pulled her into his arms. Then he gave her a hot, hard kiss. "We're more than friends, gorgeous, and don't you forget it."

He strode out of her office without looking back, mainly because he didn't want to seem as if he wanted to know how that kiss had affected her when it had shaken him to his core.

Carter knew he was playing a dangerous game with her. That he wanted something from her that she might give him, but he was trying to keep her from even knowing he wanted. He shook his head and thought of what a sap he was. He wanted to be more than friends and more than lovers, but had never in his life been successful at making any kind of relationship work.

Even his coaches had been short-term before they'd thrown their hands up and walked away. He just wasn't good at making things last. Usually that didn't bother him, but the thought of being short-term in Lindsey's life simply wasn't acceptable.

CARTER SENT HER a text telling her he'd meet her at the top of the toboggan run just after lunch. She had one more call to make, to the staff sergeant from Marietta, Montana, that Bradley had told her about.

Lane Scott was one of the men who had been part of the paraplegic ski squad. She'd heard he had recovered and was now running his family's ranch with his brothers.

"Hello, ma'am," he said, his voice deep and strong.

"Good afternoon, sir. I'm Lindsey Collins, the ski pro at the Lars Usten Resort in Park City, Utah."

"The same Lindsey Collins who broke two world records?" he asked.

No, she thought, not anymore. But she couldn't say that to him. "Yes, I am. I'm calling today because the resorts in Park City are participating in a charity event to get more kids out on the slopes, especially those who can't afford it. We're doing a kickoff event in mid-February and we were hoping some of you military guys might want to join us in the exhibition event."

"Mid-February? I think I can make it. It's not like I have to be in Marietta on Valentine's Day," he said good-naturedly. "What kind of event is it?"

"Well, I'm captaining one team and snowboarder Carter Shaw is the captain of the other one. We have local celebs and executives from the different resorts on our teams and we are each raising money for the fall event as well as getting some press for it."

"Sounds interesting. Where do my men and I fit in?"

She took a breath. "Well, your team was brought up because we know there are some kids in your situation that might not be aware they can still participate in sports. No offense. I hope you understand how I meant that…" She was feeling flustered because she wasn't sure if she'd phrased her comments right.

He chuckled. "I get it. A lot of people see losing a limb or two as the end of their outdoor life. I'd love to participate, and I think I can get one or two others to do it, as well. If it's okay with you, we'll just be a part of your two established teams. No need for us to be singled out."

"That sounds great. I'll text you my email address. Just send me your details and I'll get you all set up with the committee so you can be up-to-date on the plans. They'll assign you to a team."

"I hope I get to ski with you," Lane said.

"Me, too. I'll put in a good word. Thanks, Lane."

"Thank you for thinking of us," he said.

Lindsey hung up the phone and was moved by the

fact that Lane and his buddies hadn't let an injury slow them down. She was going to use their courage to motivate herself. And in all honesty, she was fine. So why was she struggling so hard to get back on the snow?

Once Lane's information came through, she forwarded it to the committee and then headed out to meet Carter. As she walked up the trail to the toboggan course, she put on her sunglasses and applied the lip balm of the company that used to sponsor her.

In the summer the lodge used the course, as well. It was one of the many year-round attractions that made Park City so perfect for families. But today she wasn't thinking about the fact that she had a job. Today she was thinking about her flaws. Her own shortcomings, and why other people had been able to get back on the snow and she hadn't. Her coach had sent one of his newest talents to meet with her over the Christmas break, and she suspected he'd meant it to motivate her, but all it had done was make it even harder for her to get back out there.

She wasn't young and untried. She had broken two world records and still held one of them. But she was afraid that was all in her past. It was hard to stare at your life when you were almost thirty and think that the best may have already happened. She'd always looked to each New Year as a chance to do better, to achieve more.

She saw Carter chatting with Nate Pearson, one of the guys who ran the toboggan course. Nate had been on one of the US teams at the winter games last year, so it wasn't surprising that he knew Carter.

"Hey, Lindsey," Nate said, smirking. "Couldn't believe it when this player said you were meeting him."

Lindsey rolled her eyes. Well, what could she say

in her defense? Carter *was* a player. That was why she was struggling so hard to make sure that she didn't attach too much importance to their one night together. Maybe if she was able to keep it to just that one night it might be okay. They could flirt and tease each other outside the bedroom and she could pretend that nothing had changed between them. Even though she knew that everything had.

"You're preaching to the choir, Nate. I know better than to get serious with a guy like Carter."

"I'm standing right here, you know," Carter said.

She winked at him. "I guess you are sort of charming and cute. That's why all the girls like you."

"We can't all be the Ice Queen," he muttered under his breath. "So are you ready for this?"

"Let me get you guys set up," Nate said.

He walked away, leaving them alone for a minute, and Lindsey noticed that Carter looked a bit ticked off.

"You okay?"

"Yes," he said after a long silence. "I just don't like you thinking of me as a player. That's not what I am with you."

She smiled, because he sounded so sincere. "I don't believe it's something you get to choose. You are just naturally the kind of man that all women are drawn to."

"Even you?" he asked.

Especially her. "Of course."

11

CARTER CHECKED INTO one of the residences at the resort that was away from the main building but still close enough that he could drop in when he needed to. It had been five days since he'd seen Lindsey and gone tobogganing with her. He'd contemplated buying a condo in Lindsey's development. It would have been an investment, and he did like having his own place to stay. But he had opted not to. He didn't want to push her too much. He'd been flying back and forth between professional engagements, his home in California and Park City.

He changed into some casual boarding clothes, grabbed his snowboard and headed out. He was dying to get on the slopes. He'd taken a few runs over the past few days. Not tricked-out ones as he did on the half-pipe but runs down the mountain. God, there was nothing like that feeling as he barreled down it.

He was almost to the ski lifts when he stopped and thought about Lindsey again. As if she was ever far from his mind. He knew she loved skiing the way he did snowboarding. So he went to the rental shop, stowed his board and got himself a pair of skis. He'd tried skiing maybe twice and decided he'd liked the solidness of the board beneath his feet better.

But he was going to have to sacrifice that to make sure Lindsey knew he was serious about helping her. He'd signed up for her afternoon lesson, which had already started, so he had to hurry to join the group.

He saw the look on her face when he showed up.

She forced a smile onto her face, saying, "Looks like we have a star in our midst. This is world champ Carter Shaw."

The kids all turned in his direction, and one boy, who was about eight, grinned up at him. "I wanted to snowboard, but my mom said no."

"Mom said you had to do the same thing as me and Kylie." The girl who spoke looked about two years older than the boy and, if he had to guess, Carter would have said she was his sister.

"Yeah, you're right."

"I like snowboarding but I'm a novice at skiing," he said to the kid. "We can learn together."

"Cool. I'm Jackson," the boy replied.

"Jackson, do you want to show Carter what we've learned so far?" Lindsey asked.

"Sure."

Jackson was an enthusiastic teacher for someone who wasn't sure he wanted to learn how to ski. For the duration of the class, he was Carter's shadow. Not that he minded. He followed the kid and caught up with him.

When they were all set to take their first runs down the very small slope they'd been practicing on, Carter noticed that Lindsey looked a little pale.

Was she going to ski?

Jackson went first and looked over at him, showing

off a bit as he slid down the slope and fell on his backside. One of his sisters rushed over to help him up but he pushed her hands away.

"I'm fine."

Carter used his poles and skied over to Jackson. "Dude, you did great."

"I didn't. I fell."

"Everyone falls," Lindsey said. "I crashed big time. The key is getting back up."

Carter looked at Lindsey, realizing again how brave she was. "It's not easy to do, but I bet next time your run will be even better."

Jackson nodded. Another kid called for Lindsey and she turned away to talk to the student. "Not everyone gets it the first time," he told the boy.

"The other kids seem to," Jackson grumbled.

"I'm going to let you in on a little secret, Jackson," Carter said, leaning down to look the kid straight in the eye. "I'm a slow learner. I have to practice something ten times more than other people before I finally master it."

"Really? But you've got gold medals and X-Energy girls hanging around you. Doesn't seem like you have any problems," Jackson said.

"Dude, those girls get paid to hang around me," Carter replied, realizing that the women might attract older men to the sport but were sending the wrong message to younger ones. "There are a lot of things in life, not just skiing or snowboarding, that are hard. Some of them are going to be a breeze for you and other things will be a breeze for your friends or your sister and will take you longer to master."

Carter put his poles in one hand and held his other out to Jackson. The kid reached up, and Carter pulled him to his feet. "I'm a little worried about my first run down the slope."

"We can go together," Jackson offered.

"Deal," Carter said. He glanced over Jackson's head and noticed Lindsey watching him. He winked at her.

She shook her head at him, but mouthed her thanks. "You guys ready to take your run?"

"We are," Jackson said.

Carter stayed close to Jackson as they got to the top of the slope. Lindsey skied up next to them and smiled, but he noticed the tension around her mouth. He wondered if just being on the skis was rattling her.

"Give yourself a minute to look down the slope," Lindsey said. "Remember where you fell?"

"Yeah."

"This time in your mind picture yourself going straight past there," she said.

"I will. Ready, Carter?"

"I am."

Together they took off down the slope, and it didn't really take Carter any time to adjust to having two skis under him instead of his snowboard. Lindsey had given them the basics, but more than that, just knowing the kid and Lindsey were watching was enough to make him want to do a little better.

The entire class was at the bottom of the small slope, and he looked back up at Lindsey. He was scared for her, and wondered if she'd be able to ski down it. But he saw her take a breath and come sailing down.

Her form was shaky to his eyes, but he'd seen her at her best, and today it was fear driving her—not the need to win. The smile on her face as she joined their little group, though… That was real.

THE CLASS BROKE UP and all the kids were reconnected with their parents. Jackson waved happily at Carter. Lindsey shook her head. Was there anyone who Carter *couldn't* relate to?

She sat and took off her skis, and then stood there for a minute. Her first run in the better part of a year. It was a big deal and she didn't downplay it. She'd been scared, but as usual letting Carter see any vulnerability had pushed her to just do it. And now she had. She was tempted to take another run. Down the little slope again? Or maybe something more moderate. Maybe one of the bunny slopes.

"Great class," Carter said, coming up to her.

"Yeah? Well, you were certainly a big hit. What are you even doing here?" she asked. "Ski lessons? Just doesn't seem to be your style."

"When are you going to learn that I don't fit the little mold you keep trying to shove me into?" he asked. "I'm here because if I'm going to lead a team with skiers on it, I have to at least be able to participate in a few of their events."

"Crap. Do you think I'll have to snowboard?" she asked. She didn't even want to begin to think about that. Not now. "I might give it a go on one of those indoor places. It's all virtual."

"I've seen them. In fact, I have one that is branded in my name," he said.

She laughed. Of course he did. That was really a Carter sort of thing. From the beginning he'd took to the press and to advertising as though born to it. He was photogenic, that went without saying, but he also really liked the spotlight. Almost as much as he liked snowboarding—or at least that was the impression she'd always had.

"Well, then, I guess you know what I'm talking about."

"I do," he said. "The kids in your class were great, by the way."

"You caught a good class. Some of them aren't so great. Jackson sure took to you." Lindsey looked up at him. "Don't take this the wrong way, but you were really encouraging."

"Shocked you, didn't it?" he asked with a rueful grin. "Don't let the word get out or all my rivalries will look like shams."

"As one of your biggest adversaries, I'd never let the cat out of the bag." She studied him for a long moment. "Have you ever thought about coaching?"

"It's really not my thing. I mean, helping Jackson over a learning curve is one thing, but day in, day out, keeping up that kind of energy… I'm not sure I could do it."

That was too bad. He'd sounded as though he really got the difficulties that came along with participating in a sport. Well, duh. She shook her head.

"I saw that look on your face after the run. You liked it, didn't you?" he asked.

"Sort of. When I got to the bottom, I was elated that I'd done it. But if you and the class hadn't been at the bottom, I might have walked away."

"I don't think so. You've turned a corner, Linds. You're not walking away from anything anymore."

He was right—she wasn't. She didn't know how she was going to take a big run, but from now on she wasn't going to let her fear dominate her. She'd sort of turned a corner, and she knew exactly who to thank for it.

The only problem she could see was that she'd sort of tried shoving him out of her life, but here he was again. He was one determined fellow, as her granny would say.

"Why do you keep showing up?"

"Why do you keep pushing me away?" he countered. "That's the real question. What is it about me that makes you do that?"

She could feel the heat rising to her cheeks. "I just need to sort through my stuff. And this job… I have to make some decisions, and I've always believed the best time to get involved with a man—"

"Wait. Are you actually contemplating getting involved with me? I thought I was your dirty secret. Your booty call."

She shook her head in exasperation. "I don't know why I try to talk to you. You look like a normal human being but inside you're just one big ass."

"I am. I really am," he said. "But let's both agree that you have been treating me as though I have the plague."

"You like to exaggerate, don't you?"

"Just a tad." A wicked gleam flared in his eyes. "Seriously, you *are* thinking of a relationship?"

"I don't know. Not now," she said, but that was her own pride talking. She knew that she was infatuated with him. She'd typed his name into internet search engines, read every article on him and spent hours looking at pictures of him. Especially the one of him for the famous underwear designer. It'd be dumb to pretend she wasn't already attached to him in some way.

"I can be too much," he admitted. "But it's only when I'm nervous. When I was a kid, before I found snowboarding, I used to drive my nanny crazy. Sometimes she'd have to take a day off just to keep me in line."

That was interesting. "How'd that work?"

"I wanted her to come back. She was my companion whenever we travelled and I was homeschooled for a while so I missed her."

"Why were you homeschooled?"

"I was a late reader," he said. "Isn't it funny how there is a PC term for anything that's wrong with you?"

"I bet you were too physical to actually sit still and read," she said. "Nothing wrong with that. And I'll take PC over Ice Queen any day. I can't believe Bradley called me that."

"Well, it is sort of what the media calls you. But if you want me to defend your honor, I'll challenge him on the slopes and humiliate him for you," Carter said, reaching out and tucking a lock of hair behind her ear. "Just say the word."

"I think we're good," she said with an uneasy laugh. She noticed that it was starting to get a little dark and she knew it was time to go, but she didn't want to leave Carter. Not in the punch-drunk-love way but more in a tired-of-spending-all-her-nights-alone way.

CHASING HER WASN'T working exactly the way he'd planned, but Carter wasn't going to argue with the results. Who knew that skiing would be the thing to bring them closer? In a way, that made perfect sense to him because it was the sport that had always been between them and it still was.

She'd been so focused on her skiing when they'd first met and now that she couldn't ski anymore… Well, that hadn't brought them any closer together.

"A group of people from Thunderbolt are in town and hitting a few of the bars tonight. Want to come?" he asked.

She gave him a long, level look. "Dang it. That's on my resolutions list. I guess I'm going to have to."

He knew she hadn't put *bar crawl* on her list. It was the exact opposite of everything he knew to be true about Lindsey, but he also guessed she was tired of the space between them. Or maybe that was just wishful thinking on his part. He wanted her to need him.

Almost as much as he wanted her in his bed.

"I'll pick you up at eight," he said. He knew he should go, but instead he reached for her skis and put them over his shoulder with his own. "I have to return these... unless you want to take another run."

"I was actually thinking about it. But I have to do it on my own."

"I get it," he said. "Let me trade these skis for my board and I'll catch a ride up with you and then meet you at the bottom?"

She chewed her lower lip. For a minute he understood what she'd been trying to say to him earlier. She wasn't in any position to think clearly about her future. In a way that was why he thought he had to strike now. She wasn't going to want him when everything in her life was neatly sorted into boxes. He wasn't going to fit, but he did now.

"Okay. Where's your board?"

"I left it with your staff. Someone named Jeff," Carter informed her as they walked to the main ski-rental building.

"He is a huge fan," Lindsey teased. "He probably set up an altar and lit a candle around it."

Carter had to laugh. "I doubt it."

"I don't. He talks about you and the half-pipe all the time. I guess your latest stunt has really gotten him. He'd probably love some pointers."

It always floored him when he heard someone talking about his accomplishments as though they were special. He wasn't being funny, but the stuff he did came naturally to him and always seemed just that little bit not good enough. "Maybe I'll see if he wants to meet up."

"He'd love that," Lindsey said as they entered the building. Unfortunately the kid wasn't there.

"Hey, is Jeff here? I need to get my board," Carter said as Lindsey went behind the counter to talk to the other ski instructor.

"He's going to be bummed you came back while he was gone."

"Tell him I'll stop by tomorrow... When does he work?" Carter asked. He found out and made a note in his phone to stop by. It wouldn't hurt him to chat with the guy. He worked with Lindsey, so it might even help her to see that he was so much more than his bad-boy image.

"Ready?" he asked Lindsey when he noticed she was standing by herself with her skis.

"As I'll ever be," she said.

They walked to the ski lift and waited in line to take it to the top. He could tell she was nervous because she kept looking up at the mountain. All he really wanted to do was to hold her in his arms and tell her everything would be okay. But since this probably wasn't the time or place, he searched his mind for something to distract her.

Then he grinned to himself. Humor. It worked every time.

"Oh, guess what, gorgeous? I've added a few things to my resolutions list. I might have to write a thank-you note to the resort for all the ways they are helping me improve."

She rolled her eyes at him. "What did you add?"

"Kiss Lindsey on the ski lift."

She wrinkled her nose at him. "That's too bad, because I just don't see that happening."

"That's odd. I totally do."

She laughed, but as they got closer he noted she didn't look worried anymore. When it was their turn, they both got on the lift.

"What was your best ski-lift ride?" he asked curiously.

"First time I was going up for a world event. I was so excited. I'd run the course in my mind and was so ready for it. You?" she asked.

This one. But he didn't say it. There hadn't been many times in his life that he'd done something without wondering what was in it for him. But this thing with Lindsey? Sure, it brought him closer to her and gave him a chance to tease her about kissing and intimacy, but it really was for her. She needed to be skiing, not teaching kids at a resort.

He knew that and had a feeling that she knew it, as well.

"Same. Right after I had this interview with a pretty girl and she gave me the cold shoulder."

"I guess that was a common reaction to you back in the day," she said with a grin.

"Only your reaction. I was determined to get to the top and then wow you with my skills."

She smiled. "You did when you hit the half-pipe. I've seen you run moguls, and you are good."

"Good enough to let me steal a kiss?" he asked, waggling his brows at her.

"Not today, Carter. Maybe if I make it to the bottom

of the hill, I'll *think* about kissing you good-night after we hit the clubs."

"That's a long time," he grumbled. "I'm not sure I can wait."

"I think you'll do just fine."

They'd reached the top and got off the lift. She looked over at him, and he remembered his promise. He'd had no idea it would be so hard to leave her. Especially not with that look in her eyes.

"I'm out of here," he said, but walked over to her and kissed her quickly on the lips before stepping back and putting his boots in his board. He clicked the buckles and pushed off with a grin. "You'll have to catch me to yell at me."

LINDSEY TOOK HER time getting her booted feet into her skis. The kiss from Carter... It had been nice and really not much of a surprise. His confession that he'd wanted to impress her hadn't been, either. They'd been doing that since they'd met.

She'd counted on her own feelings of not wanting to let him see her freak out to get her down the mountain. She thought of all the runs she'd taken in her life, and this one wasn't nearly the hardest or most dangerous but it was in her head.

She took a deep breath when she realized she'd been breathing in and out too quickly. She remembered New Year's Eve when he'd sat at her table and she had felt that tingle of excitement. She wanted to be that woman again.

The one who could take on anything and beat it.

She closed her eyes and offered up her little prayer, and then pushed her sticks in the ground at the same moment as she opened her eyes. She froze and forgot to crouch and was kind of awkwardly bumbling along down the slope until everything sort of clicked together.

She felt the wind on her face, and the poles started to feel right in her hands as she adjusted her stance and leaned into her run. She was skiing. *Oh. My. God.* She was on skis again and taking a run.

She didn't do anything fancy, just kept her wits about her and tried not to think of all the possibilities that were opening up to her after this. This was one of the major things keeping her in limbo, and she felt as if she'd just ripped off her last bandage and found that she didn't have a scar.

She reached the bottom of the run and skied to a stop next to Carter, who was standing there with his goggles pushed up on his head. Then she pushed hers up, too, and launched herself at him.

She caught him off guard, and he fell back onto the snow as she kissed him. Heart thudding wildly in her chest, she feathered kisses all over his face and then lifted herself up to look down into that intense blue-gray gaze of his.

"I skied."

"I saw you," he said, his voice husky.

He hugged her close, and she realized without Carter she might not be here. She looked down at him again and saw the man she'd known for all of her adult life, but she also had the feeling she was seeing him for the first time.

She'd had sex with this man, but lying in the snow on top of him after taking a run that she'd never thought she'd be able to again, she finally realized that she'd had him pegged all wrong. This was intimacy. This sharing of something that went beyond the physical.

It scared her, but it also exhilarated her, and there

was no way she was going to keep him at arm's length after this. She wasn't sure how long the magic of having Carter with her was going to last, but she intended to ride it for as long as she could.

She lowered her head and brushed her lips against his—a soft sort of thank-you to the man who'd pushed her and forced his way past all of her barriers until he got her to do the very thing that had been scaring her for way too long.

He smiled up at her, looking smug, as though he knew that he'd done something for her that she couldn't have done for herself.

"Caught ya," she said at last, reaching past him and scooping up a handful of snow.

"Dang it. Now I'm going to have to put up with more kisses," he complained.

"Not just kisses, Carter. I'm afraid you stepped over the line. I did warn you," she said, rolling over and shoving the handful of snow into the crook between his neck and shoulder.

He yelped and scooted back from her. He grabbed a handful of snow and lobbed it at her. She laughed as she unbuckled her skis and gathered more ammo to hurl at him. She kept throwing snowballs and ducking his until he rushed her. Scooping her up into his arms, he kissed her, and this time it felt real. Not a dare, not a thank-you, but that red-hot lust that always lurked beneath the surface whenever he was around.

"Enough, gorgeous," he said, letting her slide down his body and lacing his fingers through hers. "I'm proud of you. I knew you could do it, and you proved yourself."

She swallowed hard. "I didn't know I could. Thank

you, Carter. You always know just what to do to nudge me out of my comfort zone."

"I intend to do a lot more nudging tonight when we are out with my friends," he warned her softly. "I think you've been the Ice Queen for too long and you're overdue for a thaw."

She arched a brow. "I think you know that I'm not always icy."

"I do, and I like it."

They walked back to the rental building and Carter said goodbye to her. She watched him walk away, and this time he glanced back over his shoulder and winked at her before he disappeared around the corner.

12

THERE WAS ONE more week of the Sundance Film Festival in Park City, so the bars were crowded with some celebrities and a lot of film industry insiders. There were a few people she had met at the big winter games last year but Lindsey mostly avoided them. Instead she sat nestled on a high bar stool at a table jammed with people. Carter sat next to her with his arm casually draped over her shoulder.

She tried to be cool and casual, but this wasn't her kind of place and she felt uncomfortable. Plus, Carter was different here. It was as if he was aware of an image he had to project, or maybe a person he had to be, and he wasn't acting like himself.

If she'd been aware of that, she would have turned him down when he'd invited her to come along with him today.

Oh, who was she kidding? She would have been here anyway, because this afternoon after she'd skied she would have said yes to anything. There had been such a rush of adrenaline flooding through her, making her feel lighter than air.

That she could do anything.

"Another drink?" the cocktail waitress asked.

"Manhattan, please," Lindsey said.

"Vodka and Thunderbolt," Carter said. "A round for the table."

The waitress nodded and moved away. She turned to look at Carter, who wore an Oxford shirt with some sort of graffiti-style art on the left side of a snowboarder doing a "crippler"—an inverted 540 spin. He hadn't shaved, but that little bit of stubble on his jaw made him look roguish, and his hair was styled in that messy, casual way he always wore it.

"We have to show the sponsors some love," he said.

"I'm not drinking an energy drink and vodka. That kind of thing makes me feel weird. I mean inside."

He leaned in close to her. In his eyes she saw a hint of the guy who'd sat in her kitchen and played cards with her, but it was just a glimpse. "Don't tell, but me, too. I just order them and then leave mine on the table."

"Why?" she asked.

He tugged her to him as he leaned back from the table. It was as if they were cocooned together with the cacophony of noise around them.

"I have to order them. It's my image."

"But kids might buy into it. And they think you love those drinks, so they try it…"

"Damn. You're right." He winced. "But I can't change who I am now."

"Why not?"

"Because Stan and his company pay me a lot of money to do what I do. And I like it."

"So money makes it okay?" She was pushing because she was uncomfortable, she knew that. Maybe she should just let it go. Smile and be like the scantily clad energy drink girls, but she couldn't.

"Do you get off on being a buzz kill?" he asked.

"No. Sorry if my pointing out the truth is messing with your fun." She huffed.

"It's not," he said. "I'm just having a hard time being my usual self tonight."

She rubbed her finger over his stubble, liking the way it abraded her skin. She sat there thinking about her life and this year. Three weeks into January and already it felt as though things were changing.

"Maybe that's not a bad thing," she murmured. "I wasn't trying to slam your choices, Carter. Lord knows I've made a few of them that haven't been the best. I guess I'm feeling out of place so I'm not being my nicest."

He had the prettiest eyes, she thought. Especially when he leaned even closer and she noticed those little blue flecks in his irises.

"I like it when you're not all nicey-nice," he admitted. "And when have you ever made a bad choice? My entire amateur career I've heard how perfect Lindsey Collins is."

She doubted that. Her coach had pointed out every little flaw she had on every run she'd ever taken. Her mother thought her hair was too long. Her sponsor—a manufacturer of a beeswax-based lip balm—thought she needed to look Nordic and had asked her to wear blue contacts for her last photo shoot.

"Well, I'm far from perfect," she informed him. "And I have many regrets."

"Like what? Name one."

She sighed. "The things I regret most are maybe not

living as much as I should have. I mean, I'm almost thirty, and my twenties were spent training every day."

"I can't believe you regret that. Maybe because of the way your career ended you think you should have done something different…" Carter said.

Their conversation was just starting to get interesting, but their drinks arrived and he got pulled into a conversation with a Thunderbolt energy drink representative.

"Carter Shaw is hot, isn't he?" a tall, svelte redhead said as she sat next to her at the table.

"Yeah, he is. He knows it, too," Lindsey replied, turning toward the other woman. "You're Georgina Poirier, right? Stan's wife? I'm Lindsey, by the way. I saw you with Stan earlier but you and I haven't had a chance to meet."

They shook hands. "Nice to finally meet you," Georgina said. "And you're right—Carter does know how good-looking he is. I think that's part of his appeal."

Lindsey had to agree. Confidence was very attractive.

The rest of their group filed in, and Georgina left to chat with one of the Hollywood starlets who'd had the lead in the film screened at the film festival earlier today.

Lindsey slowly sipped her cocktail, feeling oddly out of sorts. Truth was, she wasn't enjoying this party as much as she had the one on New Year's Eve. It suddenly dawned on her that the reason was that she didn't have Carter's undivided attention. Then the band started playing, and the song was that catchy Pharrell Williams' tune "Happy."

She grabbed Carter's hand before she could think twice about it. "Dance with me."

He smiled at her and followed her out onto the dance floor. Moments later, when he pulled her close and they swayed to the music, moving their bodies together, Lindsey finally knew why she was here tonight. Finally, she admitted to herself that this was what she'd missed and what she craved.

She wrapped her arms around his broad shoulders and told herself that it was the only the music and the nighttime influencing her, but she had a feeling that she was lying to herself. Knew that she wanted Carter all the time, not just after midnight.

CARTER WAS FLYING HIGH on energy, and not the kind supplied by the Thunderbolt energy drink company. Stan and Georgina had left and he was free to do whatever he wanted. Lindsey was in his arms, the club was jumping and, as far as he was concerned, life was about as good as it could be.

He thought of what she'd said earlier about missing out on her twenties. In a way he'd done the same thing, but he wouldn't trade it for anything. Without that decade of really hard work he wouldn't know Lindsey and wouldn't be holding her tantalizingly close at this moment.

And she felt so good.

The music played on, and the two of them stayed on the dance floor for most of the night. She seemed lost in the music, and the moment they gyrated to the hip-hop beat until he couldn't resist her for another second. He pulled her off the dance floor and into the first quiet corner he could find.

He trapped her between the wall and his body. She wrapped her arms around his neck and pulled him closer to her until they were pressed together. Her breasts rubbed his chest; her thigh twisted around his leg. Her mouth under his, she kissed him in a way that made every other high he'd experienced in his life pale in comparison.

There was magic in her kiss, and he felt caught under her spell. She was tall, so he didn't have to bend to meet her mouth, and she never left any doubt that this embrace was hers. To the world it might seem as though he was surrounding her, but she'd been invading him body and soul. She'd taken up residence in those empty places inside him and he didn't question it.

Only wanted to let her have her way with him. Not just physically but emotionally, too. She made him want to be a better man. The kind of man that she'd be proud to call her own.

He knew they weren't close to being a couple, but he also knew that until he made a few changes she'd never want him to be her man.

But for tonight he was happy enough to let that go. To just let his hands slide up and down her torso, caressing her through the blouse she wore. She moaned and bit his lip with delicate force.

He groaned as all of his blood rushed to his groin, and he knew that every shred of logical thought was gone. Gone for the night at least, but maybe longer because this was Lindsey and all she had to do was to crook her little finger and he would follow her wherever she led.

That was dangerous. But it didn't matter. All he wanted to do was to keep kissing and caressing her. To do whatever he had to do to stay right there in her arms.

He lifted his mouth from hers, buried his fingers in her soft, silky hair and dropped kisses on her neck. He felt her fingers moving over the tattoo on his neck, and then her mouth was there, her tongue tracing the lines, and then she suckled at the base of his neck as she arched her body against his.

He thrust back before realizing that things were getting out of hand. This was Lindsey, not the kind of girl he wanted to screw in the hallway of a bar. He pulled back but she held on to him.

"Let's get out of here," he said.

She seemed startled when she realized they were still in the club. She nodded, and they went back to the table to grab their coats before weaving through the crowd to get outside. He thought the cold January air would help cool him down, but it didn't.

Not for Lindsey, either. As soon as they were out of the doorway and in the puddle of darkness between the streetlamps, she pulled him back into her arms.

He went willingly, holding her to him with his hands on her butt, anchoring her firmly to his growing erection. Her mouth moved over his, her tongue rubbing over him, and he couldn't help but rub sinuously against her in the same motion.

These weeks without Lindsey had been too long. He was trying to remember his plan. He wanted to be more than a hot lay for her, but right now his body didn't care and his mind was outvoted.

He braced his hands on the wall on either side of her head and seduced her slowly with his mouth. She pushed her hands inside his coat, caressing his chest and moving lower. She stroked him through the fabric of his jeans, her hand moving up and down, and she tore her mouth from his to look up at him with eyes dilated with passion.

"I want you," she said. "You make me forget everything except what you feel like inside me."

He shuddered and almost came right then. He needed

her desperately. But not out here on the street. He stepped back, grabbed her hand and led her to the parking lot where he'd left his SUV. He opened the door and lifted her onto the seat. She pulled him into her arms, wrapped her legs around his hips, and he thrust against her once.

"Get your seat belt on, gorgeous. We need to get home in record time."

She nodded and he closed the door, going around to the driver's side as quickly as he could. He stood there for a minute, looking up at the stars as he took several calming breaths. But the fire she'd started in him wasn't about to be abated.

He got behind the wheel and she put her hand on his thigh, moving closer to his erection. Pulsating with need, he let her caress him as he drove through the town, thankful the traffic was light.

LINDSEY FOLLOWED CARTER into his hotel room. He held her hand loosely, but the drive from the town to the lodge hadn't lessened her passion. Today had been another one of those points where she knew there was no going back to her old life. They'd happened at different times—the first when she'd been invited to train with the national team and had move out of her family home at twelve.

But this was different. This was Carter and that hot, hard sexy body of his. She wanted to make it about sex. To balance out the developing feelings she had with him and try to manage it. To lessen the impact of what he was coming to mean to her.

He dropped his keys on a table near the door and hauled her against him. She stopped thinking. Instead she felt as though she was right back in his arms with the electric pulse of the music surrounding them. She grabbed the sides of his shirt and pulled him closer to her, arched her body against his as she had earlier and lifted her head to meet his mouth, which was coming down to claim hers.

He let her take control just as he had before, and she felt a trickle of warmth flow inside her. Felt everything feminine that had once been buried beneath being an athlete now rising up and taking over. She devoured his mouth as she rubbed her hands over his chest and found the buttons of his shirt. She had it undone and pushed off his shoulders in less than a minute.

She caressed his shoulders and down his arms, feeling them flex as he wrapped an arm around her waist and lifted her off her feet. He was strong. Stronger than she'd expected him to be. She wrapped her fingers around his biceps as he set her on her feet and flexed his muscles again.

"Like my guns?"

She nodded. She continued caressing his bare chest as he flicked on a lamp on the nightstand and she realized they were in his bedroom. She undid his jeans and pushed them down his legs, wanting him naked. Needing to keep this in the context that she'd tried to assign it. She didn't want to notice the picture on his nightstand of the two of them from New Year's Eve. Didn't want to admit that this was so much more than just sex.

But it was too late. A flood of emotion washed over her. Gratitude for how he'd seen past her ice-queen facade and lust at seeing his face harden with desire for her. He wanted her. He made her feel as if she was the only girl in the world. And that shouldn't make her heart feel fuller...but somehow it did.

She pushed him backward and he fell onto the bed.

She pulled her shirt up over her head and tossed it aside, then shimmied out of her jeans and underwear. He lay on the bed naked and staring at her. There was something on his face; a quiet emotion that she couldn't identify. She knew that he was used to women.

The way he'd driven here at that high speed worried her, dimmed a little of her joy. But she pushed that aside. He wasn't a saint. He was a man.

Human, with all the faults that went with that. And he wanted her.

"Are you going to just stand there?"

"For a minute. It's not often that I can enjoy you naked and quiet. Totally at my mercy."

"Gorgeous, you've got about three seconds before I'm going to lose it and have my way with you."

She smiled at him and climbed onto the bed, straddling his lean body. She sat on top of his thighs. "Is this better? More what you had in mind?"

"Hell," he growled. "It's better and it's not."

He reached up for her breasts, cupping them in both of his hands, and she arched her back, thrusting them at him. Then she slid up his body until she could rub her moist center over his long, hard erection. It felt good as she rocked against him, and he shifted his hips, thrusting up toward her.

Pulse fluttering in her throat, she leaned over him and fused her lips with his. He pushed his tongue into her mouth, and she sucked hard on it as she rocked her hips and felt the tip of his cock at the entrance of her body. She slipped down just a bit so that he was barely inside her and moaned at the feeling. At the anticipation of being filled by him. And then she spread her thighs and glided all the way down on him until he was deeply seated inside her.

His hands slid to her waist, and he lifted his back off the bed, finding her nipple with his mouth as she moved on him. Pulled them both deeper into the web of lust and arousal. She leaned back, bracing her hands on his thighs as she continued to move.

He suckled harder at her breast and then bit lightly at her nipple, and she felt the first fingers of her orgasm shivering down her spine. She arched more frantically against him. Trying to take him deeper until everything inside her clenched and she climaxed hard. He pulled his mouth from her breast and thrust up into her three more times before she felt the warmth of him fill her.

She wrapped her arms around his shoulders, still moving her hips against his as they both slowly came down. He held her close, his hands tangling in her hair as he kissed her until their breathing slowed and they both returned to themselves.

Falling on his side, he cuddled her close. "I've missed you."

13

THE ADMISSION SLIPPED OUT, but Carter didn't want to take the words back. Deep down he had missed her and the realness he experienced when he was with her. He knew that it would be easy to say he could be himself around her, but that wasn't exactly true. With Lindsey he could be the man he wanted to be. He didn't have to be on his guard with her.

True, they competed, but with her it felt good. As though they were both doing it from a kind place, unlike some other people in his life.

"You have?" she asked.

"Never mind," he said, getting up from the bed and going into the bathroom. When he came back a few minutes later, she was sitting on the side of the bed looking at the picture of the two them.

"Where did you get this?"

"The hotel gave it to me," he said. "If you'd stuck around that morning you would have seen it."

She pursed her lips. "True. Why is it on your nightstand?"

"Because I like it," he said curtly. He'd already said

he missed her—what else did she want from him? To admit that he felt something for her he'd never experienced in any of his other relationships? He knew that was the truth, but telling her wasn't exactly something he fancied doing.

"Fair enough. And I'm sorry for what I said, Carter. I've…missed you, too. I think you scared me when you said it," she admitted. "Because the truth is, I've been thinking about you too much."

"And why's that a bad thing?" he asked, moving to sit next to her. Nothing was easy with her. And a part of him thought that was probably the way it should be. His father had always espoused the fact that value was only placed on the things he had to work hard to have. But just this once, he wanted Lindsey and him to have something easy.

"It just is," she said. "Like I've said before, I'm figuring out a bunch of stuff. Each day, even over these past two weeks, I can feel myself changing. And you're part of it. But none of it is real. It's that discovery of a life I'd thought I'd lost. But I'm also trying to find a new path."

When she gazed up at him, he could see a glimmer of uncertainty. Yet he saw hope and tenderness, too.

"And what I feel for you is strong. I meant it when I said I've spent a lot of time thinking about you."

"Me, too. That's why we can take this one moment at a time. Pretending we don't want each other or that this is never going to happen again is ridiculous. And if I know one thing about us, it's that we don't make dumb decisions."

"Speak for yourself," she said with a grin. "I'm not sure about being a team. You and me. I'm so used to being on my own."

"We wouldn't be a team per se, we'd be dating. We'd be a sort of couple."

"*Sort* of couple?" she asked. "How does that work?"

"However we want it to," Carter said. He knew himself well enough to know that he didn't do well with rules. He always wanted to break them. But with Lindsey he wanted to take things slow. No rushing in and just jumping. That was why he'd been careful about keeping his distance when he'd needed to and being himself around her.

"Okay, but just know that I might have to put distance between us. Skiing has always been my main focus, and I'm close to getting that back. I don't know how to balance anything with skiing."

He understood that. He'd known her for a long time, and she'd always been one of those people not distracted by the spectacle of international games or tempted to cavort with athletes from other countries. She'd gone to bed early, eaten well-balanced meals and skied.

That was it.

"I thought you wanted to maybe change that. Remember how you mentioned that your twenties were a blur?"

She nodded. "I do, Carter. But it has to be for me. If I figured out anything over the past year, it's that trying things for other people doesn't make me happy. And it's also not real." She blew out a breath. "I have to figure out skiing for myself, but I want you, too. I like this hot little thing we have and I don't want to lose it. Can you be okay with that?"

No. Hell no. "Sure. Whatever you need. I'm not a serious kind of guy anyway."

Liar.

He had turned into the biggest fraud…and why? She

had just said she didn't want anything serious. He knew this was karma. This was payback for all the times when he'd played fast and loose with a woman's feelings. And it sucked.

He was tired of talking, and would love for just a few moments to hold her in his arms and pretend that the facts he knew weren't real. Pretend that she was his and he could be with her all the time, not just in this unique little sliver of time when her guard was lowered and he was so desperate he'd say anything to keep her.

So he gave in to temptation.

He pulled her into his arms, tucked them under the covers, and she turned on her side to cuddle close to him. He stroked his hand over her hair as she rested her head over his heart and he felt the minute exhalation of her breath over his skin.

He knew this wasn't real. That it was a chimera of the one thing he craved most in the world at this moment, but he didn't give a damn.

She tipped her head and he looked into her sleepy brown eyes.

"I've missed you, too," she whispered. Then she lifted her head, dropped a quick kiss on his chest and went to sleep.

He lay awake until dawn crept in with its pinky-pearl color. In a way he felt as though he had everything he wanted in his arms, but at the same time she felt farther away than ever.

CARTER ASKED HER to put on the mask and get into his SUV. Given that he liked to play little bedroom games, she wasn't too sure what to expect.

"Are you going to ask me to take my clothes off?"

"Not yet," he said with a chuckle.

She felt his hands on her waist, and then he leaned over her, pulling the seat belt into position around her. She heard the door close, but all of her senses were hyperalert. She felt the breeze wrap around her the moment he opened the driver's door, heard the sound of the cloth of his jeans against the leather seats.

"No peeking," he warned softly.

"What are you doing?"

"I'm kidnapping you."

"Will there be a ransom note? My folks already think you are something of a bad boy."

He laughed, and she was reminded of how much she liked the deep timbre of his voice.

"No note. This is just between you and me. I'm sure we can come up with something for you to do in order to achieve your freedom."

"I'm not sure where you are going with this, Shaw, but I'm game," she said. And she was. She'd checked her inhibitions at the door when, almost a week and a half ago, she'd gone with Carter back to his place from the bar. Ever since then, they'd played sexy games with each other, trained with their teams for the big charity event kickoff and pretty much lived in limbo the way she had been for the better part of the past year.

The only difference was that Carter was with her now.

He put the SUV in gear, and at first she tried to keep up with the turns he made but soon realized she didn't know Park City or its surrounding area as well as she thought she did. He had some blues music playing on the radio, and the heat was cranked up, so she wasn't cold.

"Can I get a hint about this place?"

"You're going to be cold at first, but then you'll warm up and be hot and wet," he said in a deep, husky voice.

The images that came into her head were of the two of them kissing and making out in the little clearing where he'd taken her on New Year's Day. She still remembered that kiss in the snow and how it had changed everything for her.

"I get the cold, but hot and wet? Give me another hint."

"It'll feel like the Caribbean," he said. "But we're not flying anywhere."

He really wasn't helping her to figure out where they were going. "I guess I'll have to wait and see. What will we be doing there?"

"Something daring from your resolutions list," he teased.

"I hope it's not a cheese tasting," she said, wrinkling her nose. "I told you I'd start eating cheese when I'm ready."

He laughed. "No, not at all. That's one thing I'm happy to let you explore on your own."

Not cheese. She had put "try something new" on her list, but she had no idea what it would be. She racked her brain, thinking hard…then inspiration struck. It was something Elizabeth had mentioned just the other day. So why not borrow a page from her book?

"Carter, have you ever heard of picking a word for the year?" she asked. "Kind of a resolution, but more an attitude thing."

"I haven't, but it sounds intriguing," Carter said. "What word would you pick?"

"Something about returning to myself. But that sounds lame-o, doesn't it? Something better—maybe *rejuvenate*? Great, now I sound like a spa. What about you?" she asked. Surely he'd have an idea of something that might help her come up with a better word.

"Different," he said.

"Different? How?" She couldn't see how he'd done anything different this year from the years before. Except that he had retired from amateur snowboarding and had entered the professional realm.

"Just my attitude. Experiencing things that I wouldn't have before," he said. "I'm not sure how else to explain it."

She reached out and fumbled until she found his thigh and squeezed it. "I like it when you let me see the vulnerability behind that big ego of yours."

He put his hand over hers and squeezed. "That's your imagination, gorgeous. I'm always confident."

"Really?" she asked, but then chided herself. Of course he was. He hadn't fallen. He wasn't flawed and scared the way she was. He was decorated with his tattoos and his badass, can't-be-stopped attitude. In a way she resented him for that strength, but she knew that really she wanted it for her own. She wanted to claim it and find her way back to the top of the mountain instead of being on the bottom in a crumpled heap.

"Yes, really. If I feel myself slipping and doubt starts creeping in, I immediately push it out. I do the same with most of my emotions." There was a pause. "Well, the ones I can't control," he qualified.

She realized she was asking him questions she never would have if she wasn't wearing the blindfold. There was a freedom at not being able to see. It kind of made her forget her fears. In the dark she could divulge her secrets and ask him about his.

"What kind of emotions?" she asked softly. "I mean, I'm the Ice Queen, but even I can't keep my emotions locked up forever. That's why I don't usually get involved with anyone."

"That makes sense. It's easier to control them when you just don't experience it. But I have a quick temper and am passionate about a lot of things, so every day if I'm not careful I can be up and down." He tightened his grip on her hand. "That's one thing I like about you, by the way," he said.

"That I make you calm?" she quipped. "Must be my icy powers spreading."

"Nah, you make me want to impress you, so controlling my emotions is easier when I'm around you."

She liked that. Liked that she had an influence over him. Seemed only fair, since had a huge influence over her. She wasn't sure when it had happened but suspected it was that first day he'd taken her to the sledding hill. It made her feel as though, despite the way their relationship had started, it might have the seeds of something that could last. Ah, she hadn't seen that coming, but she did want this to last.

More than she dared to admit.

CARTER PULLED INTO the parking lot of the Homestead Crater near Park City. He'd seen this place on the internet a few weeks ago and had decided it would be a nice surprise for Lindsey. The past several days with her had been great, but most of the time he'd felt as if they were both working on getting her back on the slopes or training their teams. There was no time to just hang out and enjoy each other.

And he really wanted the chance to do that.

He turned off the engine and leaned over to kiss her. She'd been sitting there with the blindfold on, boldly asking him questions and sharing bits of herself that she normally wouldn't have. He had to remember that the blindfold seemed to work like some sort of truth serum where she was concerned.

"We're here, Linds."

"Great," she said, reaching for her blindfold.

She pulled it up over her eyes, and he was close enough that he saw her pupils dilate in the light. "Where's here?"

"Homestead Crater."

"I've never heard of it," she said, looking around the parking lot. "Looks like a hotel."

"It is. We're going to snowshoe to the crater, where they advertise ninety-five-degree water."

"Sounds like fun, but I don't have a bathing suit," she said.

"I brought one for you. I don't suppose you feel like changing in the front seat?" he asked casually. "I won't look."

"Somehow I'm not buying that. I'm sure they have a facility in the hotel.'

"It won't be as much fun," he said. "What if you put the blindfold back on? Would you do it, then?"

She laughed, and he bit his lip to keep from smiling. He liked seeing her forget about all the troubles of the past year. She seemed a lot like the woman he used to know before her crash.

"No. I'm not going to get naked in the front of your SUV, Shaw, so stop asking."

"Fine, be that way," he grumbled. "Just so you know, I was willing to do it, too."

"I bet. You are willing to get naked anywhere." She narrowed her eyes at him. "I saw some of those photos on the internet."

"What photos? Did you Google me?"

She clapped a hand over her mouth and shook her head.

"You did. Why did you do that?"

She shrugged. "Those two weeks I didn't see you I sort of missed you."

"Missed me? Well, I never thought I'd see the day," he said. "Tell me more."

She scooted back toward the door. "I thought we were over. I'm used to seeing more of you, and I just typed your name in once."

"Once? Surely more than that," he said, taunting her.

"Stop it, your ego can't take much more inflation. It was interesting reading the articles about you. I've never read that much of my own press. Have you read yours?" she asked.

He shook his head. He didn't mind press interviews and the like because it was the only way to get his sport more into the public consciousness, which they needed if it was going to continue to grow. But he never read it. When he'd first started, he'd read a few articles where they'd twisted his words totally out of context. He couldn't get them to change what they'd printed and had made a conscious decision to stop reading the stuff after that.

"I haven't. But I have read the articles about 'Skiing's Favorite Ice Queen,'" he said.

She flushed and shifted on her seat to put more distance between them. "I'm not anyone's favorite this year."

He put his hand on her shoulder and used his other hand to tip her face up toward his. "You're my favorite, gorgeous."

"You're just saying that because you think it might soften me up and maybe I'll get naked in your SUV," she said.

He laughed as though he could tell she wanted him to. But he knew he'd been serious. She was his favorite. He who'd never allowed himself to hold on to anything—or anyone—wanted her. Desperately. He'd always had the feeling that his life was like quicksilver, always changing, and he'd gone with the flow. But right now he wanted to pull her into his arms and never let her go.

He needed her with him, but that made him weak, and he wasn't going to be weak. There had to be a way to keep her close without losing himself. He shoved his feelings down as he always did and smiled.

Then he kissed her. A soft, slow, sweet kiss that he hoped showed her the emotions he'd never admit he had. But he wanted to. Not for the first time, he wished he was a different kind of man. Someone who would easily be able to share what was in his heart.

But he wasn't. He never had been. That just wasn't his style. And he had the feeling it might never be.

"We should go in and get changed so we're not late," he said after finally releasing her. "The person I spoke to said the guide left for the crater promptly." He opened his door, grabbed the bags from the back he'd put in earlier and handed one to Lindsey as she came around to his side. They walked into the hotel and he watched her enter the change room.

A few minutes later as they snowshoed out to the

crater, he wondered if they looked like a couple to the other people on the tour.

She didn't say much and neither did he. Part of him wanted to believe they were both just enjoying the majesty of the Utah winter, but another part knew that too much had been said.

He wasn't good at sharing, because every time he did, it ended up this way; further away from Lindsey than he had been before.

14

WHEN THEY GOT to the crater, Lindsey caught her breath. It was spectacular. The water was actually about seventy-five feet from the opening in the crater, and getting down to the water had been tricky. But now that they were here and the instructor was explaining the diving safety information, she couldn't contain her excitement.

She looked over at Carter and he smiled back at her. They were both treading water, and it was warm. Almost hot. It felt surreal being here with him.

They spent the next hour diving in the crater, and she saw some of the most spectacular sights of her life. Carter stayed next to her. A few times he reached out to tap her arm to point out the sunken wagon wheel and fake mermaid she might have missed.

While there weren't any fish due to the high calcium content, the dome over the cavern filled it with light. The crater was in the shape of an hourglass, and Lindsey followed the rugged arc of the walls. As she dived beneath the surface, she saw the chunky white surface of the wall that jutted out.

Finally they surfaced to sit on the edge of the pool

while the rest of their group finished diving. She looked over at Carter. His hair was rakishly slicked back, eyelashes thick and dark from the water, his body long and lean; she felt a spear of desire go straight through her.

If they were alone, she'd be tempted to climb onto his lap and start kissing him and not stop until he was buried deep inside her and she was riding him to completion. She blushed at the thought and felt the heat move up her neck and face.

"What are you thinking?"

"Nothing," she said. "This was a great idea."

"Thanks, but I'm pretty sure you have something on your mind besides diving," he drawled.

"I might, but it will have to wait. Unlike you, I'm not into exhibitionism."

"Who said I was?"

"*GQ* winter issue two years ago. It was on your turn-ons," she said.

He cocked a brow. "You read that?"

"I did. How else would I know that fact?"

"I just said that because the reporter was irritating me," he admitted. "I'd had a big fight with my board sponsor and it was pretty public and he kept trying to get me to bad-mouth them, which I wasn't going to do, so I said that instead."

She put her hands back on the tile behind her. Their worlds were weird. In one way they spent all their time training and trying to be the best in their sport, and then had to deal with sponsors and media. It was hard to balance it all, and she envied how Carter had always seemed to manage it.

"That was a clever way of keeping him from asking

about it. Plus, it probably got a bunch of new women to watch your sport," she said.

"Well, it didn't hurt," he responded. "Our sport has been like the bastard of winter sports for so long I'll do whatever I have to do to get more people interested in it."

"You're very outspoken. I remember when you first showed up at the training center and all the coaches weren't sure how to take you guys," she said. "You snowboarders were a group of really young athletes and coaches. No one really knew what you'd be doing." She paused. "But you've been a vital member of the winter sport family and have even brought some new events like ski moguls into the sport."

"It has been a long, hard fight," he agreed, "trying to get some respect."

"Why'd you do it?" she asked curiously.

"I like recognition as much as the next guy. My dad was impressed when I got my gold medal," he said. "Plus, I liked being part of the team that represented our country."

"Me, too. Most of the time I don't think about being from the US, but when we walked into the opening games and the anthem played, I really felt it. I wanted to win not just for me but for everyone back home."

He smiled at her. In that moment she realized there was a lot more to Carter Shaw than he wanted the world to see. He seemed like this tough badass, but in truth he was a softie just like her.

Their tour guide gathered them together for the hike back to the hotel. This time Lindsey didn't seem as distant from Carter as she had been on the way down. She reached for his hand and held it in hers as they walked back.

After they'd changed and she headed out to meet him

in the lobby, she noticed he was talking to a group of people but stopped when he saw her.

He waved goodbye to the group and walked over to her. He made her feel special. As though, despite her flaws and scars, she was enough for him.

IN THE WEEKS that followed their diving at the crater, Lindsey felt they'd fallen into a safe routine. She got up each morning and took a run down the bunny slope. Each time she felt paralyzed with fear at the top, but when she got to the bottom she felt exhilarated. She often met her friend Elizabeth for breakfast and then worked her shift at the school.

Carter was always in one of her classes. She wouldn't admit it to anyone, but she was starting to really care for him, and that worried her. This new life where she could only ski the easiest slope and where Carter was part of her joy was odd, but she liked it.

It was time for her last class of the day, and she skied out to meet the kids, a little disappointed when Carter wasn't there. Though he hadn't said he'd be at the class, this would be the first day he'd missed. These kids had been taking lessons for a while, and most them already had the skills they needed to ski. They were ready for something more advanced, as was she. She felt nervous, but made the decision after checking with their parents to take them to the ski lift for a moderate run.

This would be her first chance to try out something other than the bunny slope. She was nervous, of course, but having the kids along made her focus on them and not herself.

"This kind of thing must seem pretty tame to you,"

Courtney said as they got off the ski lift and readied to take their run down the mountain.

"Not at all. I love skiing, and when I'm on the snow I'm just happy to be there," she said. The words were press friendly and sound-bite worthy, but she realized that she meant them. This was what she'd needed.

And she didn't need Carter Shaw to do it. Not that she ever had, but she realized she'd sort of been leaning on him as a crutch.

Dan, one of the other instructors, had come along for the run and taken the first group of kids down the slope. The ski patrol was nearby and always on alert, so she wasn't worried. These kids were good skiers. She was more concerned her nerves might snap, but her fear of embarrassment was greater than her fear of a fall, and as she led the last group down the mountain, she felt a little of her old confidence returning.

She hadn't realized how much she'd missed it until this very moment. And when she got to the bottom, she knew that something significant had changed inside her. Everything was telling her to go to the top and take a run.

Lindsey released a sigh. She was a little freaked out that she hadn't heard from Carter all day. And there had been no answer to the texts she'd sent earlier. She wanted to take her run, but now she was worried about Carter.

This just wasn't like him.

Something had to be seriously wrong for him not to show up or to return her texts.

She stowed her skies and signed out at work. Changing out of her ski gear into a pair of faded jeans, a thick sweater and her Ugg boots, she decided to swing by his place to check on him.

But as she walked into the lodge and up the patio, she noticed a large group around the pools and hot tubs. Looked like a camera crew, even. They were probably filming a new commercial for the resort, but as she looked closer she recognized a couple of Thunderbolt women from the shindig at the bar a while back.

She started for the group, thinking maybe they knew where Carter was, when she saw him. Sitting in the middle of the hot steaming water with his arms around two bikini-wearing hotties. Her heart sank. She'd heard that expression before, but this was the first time she'd actually experienced it.

She felt light-headed, as though she wasn't all there, and then she felt her face turning red. This was so embarrassing. She'd been worried about him. She'd given up skiing to come find him because she'd thought that surely something must really be wrong.

And he was sitting in a hot tub with a bunch of women!

His laughter rang out over the pool area, and she clenched her fingers together. She felt stupid. As though she should have known this would happen. As though the relationship she'd thought they were building was just a thought on her side.

She almost went to confront him, but then Georgina caught her eye, and the look of sympathy on her face made Lindsey feel so small she just turned and walked away.

She didn't want to think about Carter Shaw. She got as far as the lobby where Elizabeth was talking to one of the front-desk staff. Her friend waved, but something on Lindsey's face must have showed her inner turmoil because Elizabeth rushed over.

"Are you okay?"

"I'm great," she said through clenched teeth.

"Uh, let's go get a drink and talk." Elizabeth wrapped her arm around Lindsey and led her to the bar.

Lindsey could only nod. She needed someone to talk to, and hadn't realized how much until this moment. She was used to keeping everything inside. Had made her reputation in skiing by being the Ice Queen… Maybe it was those months when she'd been here working and not practicing, but suddenly it felt as if she had no control over her emotions anymore.

She didn't like it, but she couldn't change it.

"What's up?" Elizabeth said once they had secured two empty seats in a corner of the cocktail lounge. "You look like… Well, if it was anyone else I'd say you look pissed off."

Lindsey nodded tersely. "I am."

"At who?"

"Carter Shaw."

CARTER HAD HAD a really long day, and when he was finally free of the corporate people his first thought was to go find Lindsey. She'd become his touchstone. The calmness in his crazy world. He'd hoped to make it to one of her ski lessons today but was disappointed he'd missed out on it.

"Hey, Carter, you got a minute?"

Georgina was one of Thunderbolt girls, though calling her a girl was a bit of a misnomer. She was his age and had been married to Stan Poirier, the owner of the Thunderbolt energy drink company, for a few years now. He liked her—she was nice enough and had always sort of had a way of making the overtly sexy ads he shot for her husband's company seem almost okay.

She also must have the temperament of a saint to put up with Stan's flirting. But there was some real love between those two, and somehow they must have figured out something that worked for them.

Carter wanted that with Lindsey. But he was honest enough to admit that he had no idea how to get it. He wasn't good at the normal days. He could do nights of sex and fun adventures, but the everyday living was harder.

"Actually, I was just on my way out," he said. He was anxious to find Lindsey. And, if he was honest, to wash away a bit of the fake attitude he'd had to step into to be the spokesman for Thunderbolt.

"It won't take long," she promised, leading him away from the others to a cozy couch set up in one of the alcoves in the long hallway in the lodge.

"What's up?" he asked as she sat and gestured for him to sit next to her. Sitting would mean this wasn't going to be as quick as he had hoped, but he complied.

"That woman you were with at the nightclub, Lindsey... I think she's an Alpine skier," Georgina started.

"Yes, she is. What about her?"

"She saw you filming. She didn't look too happy and I wanted to let you know before you went charging off to see her."

Ah, hell. That was the last thing he'd expected. "Thanks."

He started to stand, but she stopped him. "Do you want some advice?"

He just looked at her, and she smiled.

"Probably not, right? Who wants to listen to another

person when it comes to relationships? But I'm going to tell you about Stan and me. He's always interviewing those gorgeous girls. You know how they look at him, and he likes it. He likes that they fawn all over him."

"It's not like that for me," Carter said. "Lindsey makes all the rest of them pale in comparison."

"Good. Make sure you tell her that."

He studied Georgina for a moment. "Does Stan tell you that?"

"Not often enough," she confessed. "But I know he loves me."

"How?" Carter asked curiously. Women had sometimes mentioned the *L* word around him, but the truth was he'd never experienced it in a relationship. He loved his dad, but then the old man had been his only constant in his life. His mom had died giving birth to him, and it had always been just him and his dad. A part of him thought maybe the fear that gripped him when he thought of not having Lindsey in his life might be love.

Or maybe it was something else. He just had no idea.

"Stan shows me every day," Georgina explained. "Does special little things that he knows I like, and he always makes me feel like I'm the most beautiful woman in the world. I don't know if that will work for Lindsey, but it does for me." Leaning closer, Georgina reached out and patted him on the shoulder. "Every year those girls seem younger, and I feel… Well, that doesn't matter. I just wanted you to be aware of what she'd seen. I like her."

"I do, too. I'll explain that I had to do the photo shoot today."

She arched a brow. "You've known about it for weeks."

"I…I'm not really good with the relationship stuff," Carter admitted, releasing a frustrated breath.

"Don't try to pull that kind of BS with her."

It was funny that Georgina could see through it; most people just shrugged and assigned it to his snowboarder, live-free attitude. But she knew that it wasn't. He didn't like the fact that she could read him, and wondered if his mask was slipping now that he was spending so much time with Lindsey.

With her he felt as though he could be himself. But he didn't feel that way with the rest of the world. Certainly not with the Thunderbolt energy drink company. He needed to keep his guard up.

"I won't. Thanks," he said, standing.

He walked away from Georgina, but the farther he moved into the lodge, the slower his steps became. Talking to Lindsey wasn't going to be easy. He knew it. He should have mentioned it earlier, but he'd felt silly saying he was going to be in a hot tub with a bevy of twenty-somethings.

"Dude, you don't want to go to the bar," Bradley said, coming up behind him.

"Why not?"

"Lindsey is pissed about what happened earlier, and Elizabeth texted me to find you."

Great. "It was just a job."

"I get it, man, believe me, I do. But apparently Lindsey thought there was something wrong with you because you missed a class. She went from worrying for your safety to seeing you cavorting in a hot tub."

"Damn. I didn't think of it that way."

"Or maybe you did," Bradley said. "I know for me there are times when I need to know that I'm at least as important to Elizabeth as the resort is. So I do stuff to get her attention."

Was that what he'd been doing?

He knew each day she was getting more confident on her skis and needed him just a little bit less. That was something he couldn't tolerate.

15

"I'M SORRY," CARTER said as she opened the door to her condo. He'd texted her that he'd had to work and had just gotten her message. Then he'd asked if he could stop by her place and she'd said yes.

Lindsey was over her earlier upset and realized that if she was going to be involved with Carter she'd have to get used to seeing him with other woman. His biggest sponsor had a lot of those scantily clad girls. But she also knew that it was more complicated than that.

"It's okay. I was foolishly worried something had happened to you," she said. But it wasn't as if they'd had a standing appointment or anything like that, so a part of her felt that maybe she shouldn't have been so freaked out.

"I know. I should have mentioned the photo shoot but I just didn't... I felt like we were starting to feel too settled and that I had to tell you, so I didn't."

"It's fine. I get it." She gave him a cavalier smile. "Remember, we said we'd make up our own rules. So we don't have to share everything if you don't want to."

He stepped inside her condo, and she closed the door behind him. "The thing is, I think I want to."

Lindsey didn't believe him. She wasn't even going to pretend that his idea of being a sort-of couple could work for her anymore. He'd made it pretty plain that he wanted to sleep with her, and she liked that, but she knew that moving forward she was going to have to make sure she didn't start thinking of him as anything other than a lover.

"It's cool."

He shook his head, and she could see his jaw tighten "It's anything but cool. I was playing a game and it feels like I might have lost."

"We both did. We were both pretending that for the past weeks we lived in some sort of world where it was just the two of us. But the truth is, you still have a pro career and you need to dedicate a certain amount of time to it."

"I can see you've thought this through," he said quietly.

He leaned against the wall, and she couldn't keep the image from flashing through her mind of the last time he'd held her in his arms in a hallway. The way his mouth had moved over her lips, trailing hot, molten kisses down her neck before travelling slowly lower. How she'd lifted her arms above her head and stopped thinking.

That might have been dangerous.

She needed her wits to deal with Carter. To ensure she didn't forget the truth of who he was. Of who *she* was. While this was fun, that was all it would ever be, and she had to remember it.

She had to stop looking for him at her ski lessons and wanting to share her little successes with him. He was already putting her in one section of his life, and she needed to stay there.

"I have thought it through. I'm starting to ski a lot more. Today the class and I went down a moderate run, and I've called my coach to tell him I think I'm ready to get back to training. I don't know what the future holds for me, but I know I have to try skiing again."

"What about your other commitments?" he asked. "Your job at the resort and the charity event?"

She licked her lips and tipped her head to the side. "I'm going to take a part-time role at the resort and I'm still captaining the team. Lars thinks my return to the training should help boost our team's chances of beating yours."

He shoved his hands through his hair and exhaled roughly. "I don't want this to end."

"It's not. I'm sure there will still be moments of weakness on my part where I call you and ask you to stop by."

"Weakness?" His eyes flicked to her face.

"Yeah, weakness. I felt so upset seeing you today with those women. I get that it's your job and you're going to keep on doing it…but you didn't say anything to me about it. Didn't mention it, even though every night I talk to you all about my students."

"That's different."

"See, until today I didn't realize that." She swallowed a lump in her throat. "To me it felt like I was building toward something. Slowly pulling my life back out of the abyss where it had fallen, but then I had a wake-up call."

He moved closer to her and she stood her ground, not backing up or turning away, because this was too important. She'd hidden away from life when she'd lost her ability to ski, and Carter hadn't taken anything from her, but today she'd had a glimpse of what he could take, and she simply couldn't allow that to happen. Not again.

"What wake-up call?"

"That I'm more involved than you are," she accused. "It made me feel silly, especially when I'd thought that something must be wrong, that you'd had an accident or something. If it had been me, I would have let you know."

He cursed under his breath and turned away from her.

"Why are *you* so pissed?"

"Because you have it all wrong, Linds. I've been struggling this entire time to keep from letting you see how much you mean to me. How much I need you in my life." He turned back to her, reached for her, but she recoiled.

"What the hell…?" he asked.

"I can't think when you touch me, and I need to make sure I'm clearheaded."

"Fine. I haven't wanted to crowd you, and I guess that maybe I thought of today as a chance to see how much I mean to you," he said brusquely. "I shouldn't have done it, but I'm tired of always guessing where I stand with you."

HE SHOULD HAVE been better prepared for this but knew he had been hoping this would all blow over. It hadn't. And, in hindsight, it was probably for the best. This had been lurking under the surface for a while now for him. It had felt too unsettled. He knew that he was going to have leave Park City after the February event to kick off the charity to fulfill his Thunderbolt Extreme Winter Games duties, but he'd be coming back and forth for the next six months. He hadn't known how to ask Lindsey if she still wanted to see him.

"I'm not a coward," he said. "You're the one who's been afraid and hiding here. Not at the training center, but at a resort teaching little kids to ski."

"There's nothing wrong with what I've been doing. It takes time to recover from the kind of injury I had."

He knew that. He was just being mean because she'd cut a little too close to the truth with her comment. The fact was, he was scared. Scared of having his heart broken. He'd known he was in danger ever since they'd started sleeping together. She'd known it, too. He could tell by the way she had wrapped her arms around her waist.

"I know. That was horrible, and I have no idea how long it would take me to come back. You're sort of my hero for getting back on skis as quickly as you did," he said, shoving his hands through his hair again. "I don't want to fight with you, gorgeous."

"Me, either," she admitted. "I like you, Carter, but you've never really been serious about anything but snowboarding. Today, when I was searching for you, I realized how much you've come to mean to me."

"How much?" he asked, staring at her intently. He had to know. And he wanted her to go first and tell him that she cared so he'd feel that much safer admitting he felt the same.

"A lot. Too much," she whispered. "So much so, in fact, that somehow in my mind you and skiing have become intertwined. And that's dangerous."

He inhaled deeply. "It's like that for me, too. But I didn't want to admit it. I like all the time we've spent together and I'm scared of what will happen when I leave Park City."

He took a step toward her, and this time she didn't back away. And when he wrapped his arms around her and pressed his lips to her forehead, she didn't resist. Finally he had her where he needed her. He hugged her close and let out a small breath of relief. This was one of those little hiccoughs that couples went through. They'd get through this.

"When are you leaving?"

"Not until after our charity competition. I have other commitments that I have to fulfill...but I don't want this to end."

"Are you sure?"

"More sure than I've ever been of anything in a long time." Holding her close, he gently threaded his fingers through her hair. "It's ironic that it was me wanting to keep my professional life away from you that caused this. I've never had someone in my life that I've shared so much with before."

"Me, either," she said in that quiet way of hers.

"Can we start again?" he asked. "Third time might be the charm for us."

"How do you figure we had three times?"

"Seventeen, when I was a jerk. New Year's Eve, when you were...well, fabulous. And now this time when we are both ready."

"Okay," she said. "How about we grab dinner and talk?"

"I was hoping for something more physical."

"Sex?" she asked.

The way she said it let him know that if he said yes, it wouldn't be his smartest move.

"Not right now. I know a nice place where we can do some snowshoeing. It's not too far from here and might be perfect for tonight."

"Why?"

"Because we can forget about all the fears that are making a relationship such a struggle for us."

"Sounds perfect. Where is it?"

He pulled out his smartphone and glanced at the screen. "Not too far from here. One of these places groomed by the Mountain Trails Foundation. Ever heard of it?"

She took the phone from him and studied the screen, and he almost felt as if they might be okay. But he'd never had anyone in his life he feared losing the way he did with Lindsey. She was more than a lover.

That was hard for him to admit, but he knew it was the truth.

"I haven't. But it sounds like fun."

Suddenly his stomach growled. "Have you arranged for dinner?" he asked.

"I have a pizza on the way," she said, leading the way into her kitchen.

She got out drinks for them while he called to make an appointment. "Can you go tomorrow night?"

"I can," she said.

He finished the arrangements and the pizza arrived. They sat at her table eating and he realized that she wasn't talking. That maybe just because he'd thought everything was okay, it wasn't.

"Tell me about your lessons," he said. "I had planned to make the last one but then the shooting ran over."

Her eyes lit up. "That class was awesome. Some of the kids were getting restless—you know they are more advanced than some of my other ones—so I decided to take them on a run."

"You did? Which one?"

She gave him a smile that cut him all the way to his soul. So much joy and pride in her look that he knew he was falling for her. That her joy could be his was the first indication. But it wasn't the only one. How he'd planned to stay here until he could get back in her good graces was another one.

"A moderate one. Not a world-class trail, but it was close, and I wasn't scared this time. I mean, I was at the top, but once I started skiing it was like old times. I got into my stance and just sort of felt everything fade away."

"Gorgeous, that's great! Tomorrow morning we're going up the mountain."

LINDSEY LEFT A note for Carter to meet her and left early to meet Elizabeth for breakfast. They'd started the tradition when Lindsey had first started working at the resort and had kept it up even through the holidays and new relationships. Last night in the bar, she'd been so out of control with her feelings that she hadn't really been able to talk.

They sat in the main dining room at the lodge, the Wasatch Range standing majestically in the distance. Lindsey was playing with her food more than eating it.

"I don't think a night's sleep has helped you," Elizabeth said.

"It hasn't. If anything I'm more confused now than ever," she admitted. It was hard to talk about her feelings. She just wasn't the kind of woman who had ever done a lot of sharing.

On the team where she'd spent most of her life, everyone had been focused on their own goals. Sure, they'd discussed good runs or new products, but they'd never really talked about their real lives. Elizabeth reached over and squeezed her hand. "What's on your mind?"

"Stuff," Lindsey said. "Honestly, I can't make any sense of it. There's a part of me that wants to believe that Carter has changed, and I've changed enough to give him a shot, but then there's this other part that's too afraid to believe it. And I'm stuck not knowing which is right."

Elizabeth took a sip of her coffee. "I'm betting the truth is somewhere in between all of that. Maybe you are looking for an easy answer where there isn't one. I'm far from an expert on relationships—believe me, Bradley would be the first to say that—but I have discovered that you have to be honest with yourself, with your heart. Otherwise you will be miserable."

Lindsey took a bite of her omelet and wondered what her heart wanted. She knew she cared for Carter. She couldn't deny it after the blind panic she'd felt the day before when she couldn't find him. But love? She was afraid to admit to it. In her life she'd loved two things: her family and skiing.

Right now she was struggling to find her way back to skiing and felt as though she was on the right path. What she felt for Carter wasn't really like that. She had no idea how to define it or him. She just knew that when he'd showed up at her place last night, she'd felt a sense of relief mixed with joy.

"How do you know what the heart wants?" she asked Elizabeth. If there was one woman in the world who seemed to have it all, it was her friend. She needed some guidance here. Because she'd been out of the game of love for too long.

"Only you can say. When Bradley called me, even before we were dating, I'd get really excited. I couldn't wait to talk to him, and I pretended we were just friends and that was all I wanted, but I knew I needed more from him."

It was different for her and Carter. She'd never felt anything toward him except for faint amusement and a little bit of irritation before New Year's Eve. She'd needed this year to be different. Vastly different from last year, which, if she was completely honest, she could say was happening.

The problem was, as much as she wanted to change, she kept getting tripped up on the fact that she had no idea how to really handle it. How to handle Carter. Jealousy would have been easier to deal with, but the truth was that it had been more than jealousy she'd felt at those other women. Something deep inside her had been awakened and she'd wanted to claim him. To tell those girls and everyone else that he was hers.

And that was far from the truth.

"Thanks," she said.

"I didn't help, did I?" Elizabeth replied with a very kind smile.

"No. But I'm beginning to believe this is something that I have to figure out for myself."

"The toughest decisions are. But that's the way it should be, since you're the one who has to live with the consequences."

Consequences. She had left him this morning, and it had been hard. He was leaving soon to get back to his touring schedule and his new professional life. He'd said last night that he didn't want to lose her, but she knew him better than that.

Eventually he would move on.

And where would that leave her?

Lindsey took a sip of orange juice to wash away the parched feeling in her throat. She should put some distance between them now, instead of skiing with him and asking him to stay the night at her place.

"I guess you must really like him," Elizabeth said, "if you are that confused about what to do."

She did like him. A lot. But as with all the other things in her life that she wanted, he was right out of her grasp. He wasn't like skiing, something she could train for and master. He was always going to keep her guessing and trying to keep up with her own feelings.

She had to cut her ties to him, and she had to start doing it now.

"Sure, what's not to like? Carter is sexy, charming and just the sort of guy a woman uses as a distraction."

16

CARTER WOKE UP feeling pretty good. He'd done just enough to get Lindsey back in his bed where he wanted her. Or, as it was in this case, his bed. He saw her note and swung by his place to shower, change and collect his snowboard. Hitting the slopes with Lindsey was going to be fun.

It felt right in his bones to be doing this with her, and after yesterday's setback, he was ready to move forward. He hoped that he didn't have to talk about his emotions ever again.

That had easily been the scariest moment of his life. He smiled at the valet as he tossed his keys to him and stopped by the little counter-service café off the lobby for a coffee before heading into the main dining room to find Lindsey.

He saw her sitting with Elizabeth near one of the windows. They were talking intently, and he felt something shift and settle in his soul. She was his. Lindsey looked pretty with her long blond hair hanging loose around her shoulders. She wore a pair of leggings and a long sweater, and when she talked she gestured with her hands.

He stood there in the shadows, just watching her, almost afraid to believe that he'd somehow convinced her to take a chance on him. The guy that the world saw as never serious about anything had a very serious crush on her.

His ice queen.

He'd melted her, and in return found that she had melted him. A part of that would never be the same again.

He took a sip of his coffee as the maître d' came over to see if he wanted breakfast.

"Nah, I'm fine. I'm going to surprise those ladies."

The other man nodded, and slowly Carter made his way through the tables. There weren't that many people in the restaurant this morning. He noticed Georgina and Stan were sitting quietly together, and he thought of how it took all types of relationships. That there wasn't just one kind of relationship or one answer to how they worked.

Maybe even someone like him could find true happiness with Lindsey.

"He was a distraction," Lindsey said.

He paused. Was she talking about him?

"Are you talking about me?"

She glanced over her shoulder; all the color left her face and she bit her lower lip.

"Carter, how nice to see you this morning," Elizabeth said quickly.

But he wasn't interested in being sociable or pleasant right now. Unless he was wrong—and let's face it, he wasn't—Lindsey had pretty much just relegated him to booty-call status. Well, hell. He'd been thinking they were something special and she was getting ready to show him the door?

"We're you talking about me, Lindsey?" he asked again.

She turned her face down and wouldn't meet his gaze. "Yes, Carter, I was."

He didn't know what else to say to that. And he hadn't been expecting her to admit it—especially not in front of Elizabeth.

"I thought we were past that." He gritted the words out. "Didn't last night mean anything to you?"

She stood. "I don't want to talk about this now."

"That's too bad," he said, blocking her path. "Your *distraction* isn't going to be just brushed aside as easily as that."

"Carter, please. I don't think this is the right time."

"Too bad. I'm tired of running after you and never feeling like I'm good enough. You know that you can't keep me dancing to your tune forever."

"You haven't been dancing to anyone's tune except your own," she said, her temper flaring. There was a red flush on her cheeks as she stepped forward, pushing her finger at his chest. "We aren't normal couple material. You have a life that takes you around the world, I don't. I'm here working and trying to figure out—"

"Figure out what? How to not be afraid of the one thing that makes you special?" Sure, he had weaknesses, but she did, too. How could she not see that with her, he was different? With Lindsey he had a shot at being the man he'd always wanted to be but had never been able to figure out how.

As soon as the words left his mouth, he knew he'd

gone too far. She shoved her way past him. He wanted to take it all back. To pull her into his arms and apologize, but he couldn't. He knew he should, but he wasn't built that way. And the farther out of his grasp she moved, the meaner his thoughts became.

"Don't walk away like that," he said.

She shook her head, and he saw the sheen of tears in her big brown eyes…but she didn't let them fall. "At least I have something that makes me special and I'm not afraid to admit it."

What the hell did she mean by that? "I'm not hiding."

"Yes, you are hiding. Everything you do is another barrier to keep everyone from seeing the real man. The boy I met at seventeen already had those barriers in place, so I wonder if you even know who you really are anymore."

She'd cut a little too close to the bone with that observation, and later on he'd feel the bruising, not just to his ego but also to his soul. But right now he was too busy trying to even the score and make sure she walked away as deeply hurt as he was.

"You're not seventeen anymore, either, and maybe hiding away in Park City isn't the solution for you," he said harshly. "You fell. So what? A lot of skiers fall. You were injured and now you're better. It's time you stopped hiding."

He'd gone too far again, and this time she didn't look as if she was going to cry. Instead it seemed she might actually hit him. "Congratulations, Carter, you've ceased being a distraction and become an irritant. And one I'm happy that I am able to walk away from."

"Just like you walk away from everything else in life whenever it doesn't come easily to you," he said.

"At some point, gorgeous, you're going to have to stop running scared."

"Screw you, Carter."

LINDSEY WAS HUMILIATED, angry and hurt. She strode out of the restaurant and away from Carter and all the people who'd witnessed their argument. God knew no one was going to refer to her as the Ice Queen after that outburst.

She was shaking and felt as though she might be sick, so she sat on one of the chairs dotted along the hallway. She put her head in her hands and felt as if she wanted to cry, but the tears wouldn't come.

There were a lot of times when she had cried. The day they'd told her she'd need surgery. The day she'd gone back and found out she'd need a second surgery and a long recovery period. But this was the first time a man had made her feel this way. She wondered if she'd started the fight and pushed him away because it was easier to be alone than to figure out how to be with him.

In one preemptive strike she'd made sure she didn't have to worry about him or who he was with when he was away from her. She'd pretty much made sure she'd never have to see him or talk to him again.

It was difficult for her to clear away the anger. But once she did, she knew that if she hadn't been trying to save face with Elizabeth and called him a distraction, none of this would have happened.

She also knew that it had needed to happen. There wasn't any path for the two of them. She knew that now.

She was flawed...but that wasn't why she'd started the fight with him. She should have just been comfort-able enough to tell him how she felt. That she was riddled with uncertainty, but admitting that she didn't know what she was doing still wasn't easy for her.

Especially with Carter.

She heard footsteps, and looked up to see one of the families from her ski lessons.

"Morning, Miss Lindsey," Jeremy said.

Oh, crapola. Had they witnessed her fight with Carter? She forced a smile, grateful to have an excuse to slip behind her iron wall once again. "Morning, Jeremy. Mr. and Mrs. Smith. How are you today? Looking forward to our lesson?"

"I'm good. We are going for a toboggan ride this morning," the boy said.

"Jeremy loves your lessons," Mrs. Smith said. "I know you probably get asked this all the time, but can he take a picture with you?"

"Sure," Lindsey said.

Jeremy came over to her, and she wrapped her arm around his little shoulders and leaned in and smiled. The same fake smile she'd used for years after defeats at world-champion events. And it seemed to fool them as they smiled and waved goodbye.

She sat back in the chair and realized that if she could find away to slip back into that persona as her normal, everyday self, she'd be fine.

Yeah, right.

"So, um, maybe you were right about not talking in the restaurant," Carter said from where he stood across the hallway.

She'd been too caught up in Jeremy and his family to notice that he'd arrived. She hated that she'd said those mean things, but she knew under her anger there was a kernel of truth. For him as well, she thought.

"I'm sorry," she whispered.

"I'm not," he retorted, flashing that familiar smirk. "I put 'big embarrassing fight with Lindsey' on my resolutions list."

She shook her head. "Glad I could help. I'm good at that."

"Just like I like being a distraction," he said, coming over to sit next to her. "That hurt."

"I know. I'm sorry," she said. "It's not something I would have said to you."

He lifted a dark brow. "Then why did you say it to Elizabeth? She's my friend, too."

She knew that. She'd said it because… Those reasons didn't matter to her right now. "I don't know. I just felt it was one more thing in my life that I had no control over and I hated it." She took a breath, let it out. "It's hard to deal with the way I feel for you. I know we hashed things out last night, but this morning it feels even more messed up than ever. I like sex with you. That part feels safe and okay, but the emotions and how tied you are to my skiing… I don't like it."

"What are we going to do?" he asked.

"You could maybe not always seem like everything works out for you. You act like nothing that happens between us fazes you," she said.

"Of course it does," he admitted. "I'm always running and trying to catch you, Linds, and you are always just out of my reach."

She didn't believe that for a minute. He had been there when she needed him, seen her at her worst, and always seemed so with it and cool. As if he was rolling on through life just as he had planned.

"It doesn't seem that way," she told him quietly. "I wish you had some flaws like me."

"I have more flaws than you, gorgeous," he said. "Everyone knows that."

"You still have your career. You seem great at everything you try—even skiing—and I have to admit I was sort of hoping you wouldn't be."

"What can I say? I've always been good on the snow. You know…" Carter shrugged. "'The cold never bothered me anyway.'" He sang the line from the Disney movie with a smile. "That's why I've always been drawn to you."

He was playing again. Trying to lighten the mood…to distract her from her very real fears. She knew that was why she'd started the fight today. He wasn't just a distraction to her anymore. He hadn't been for a while, and she was afraid to admit to herself how much she needed Carter. She was serious—too serious about her life and about having him in it. Her biggest fear was that to him she was a temporary stopover. And once he moved on, she'd be left alone again.

He felt that he was losing again. Last night he'd dodged the bullet and hadn't had to bare his soul, and now it felt as if he might have shortchanged himself by not doing that. But her doubts were spurring on his, and he no longer felt as confident as he had when he'd woken this morning in her bed.

Alone in her bed.

Maybe that had been some sort of sign that he was too blind to see. He stretched his arm along the back of the seat and released a ragged breath. He wanted to hold her. To pull her into his arms, kiss her until she was ach-

ing for more and somehow fix everything that was broken between them. But he was afraid that he couldn't.

That maybe there was no way for things to be fixed
between them.

"Singing isn't your strong suit," she said at last in
that quiet way of hers that really revealed nothing of
her inner thoughts.

His lips twisted ruefully. "I guess it wouldn't be fair
if I could sing when I've got all this going on."

"Probably," she said, slouching back against the arm
of the seat and looking over at him. "What are we going
to do now?"

"I don't know," he admitted. "I want to shrug this
off and pretend that nothing happened, but we are both
wounded by what we said. I'm sorry, too, by the way. Is
there a way we can move forward from this?"

She tipped her head to the side, studying him. "Only
if you are honest with me. You said that life isn't as easy
for you as it seems. Show me the real Carter."

The real Carter. Did that man even exist? He had
been pretending for so long that he almost thought that
this guy was the real man. But he knew that he wasn't.
He knew from the way he'd been chasing after Lindsey,
that each time she walked away from him he wanted
something more.

"What's real? I want you in my life," he said.

"I know that. Why?"

How to put into words what he could barely understand as emotion. It was almost beyond him, and as he
sat there in the quiet hallway he understood for the first
time the real meaning of fear. He'd thought he'd experienced it before, but it paled compared with this. "You
know how everyone in the world has an image of you?"

She nodded.

"Well, for me, I've always seen that beyond that you were this girl who wanted something more. You weren't icy because you thought yourself above everybody." He looked into her eyes. "You were cold because unless an endeavor improved your skiing, you didn't bother with it. I liked that."

"Why?"

He sighed. "You know how everyone thinks that nothing bothers me and I just keep rolling on?"

"Yes. That's why I want to know what you feel," she said.

"Well, I am the same as you. Underneath that, I do what I have to do to get back to the important stuff. I've always thought if we ever both dropped our guard, we'd have a lot in common and be a powerful pair. I've never told anyone, but I have dyslexia. It was hard for me to overcome."

"But we can't be," she said sadly. "We'd both have to change to do that."

"Change?"

"Yes, you can't give up your persona and I can't give up mine." She sighed. "I realized that when I saw you yesterday in that hot tub."

"*That* again? I thought we had settled it."

"We did. I understand that you aren't really interested in those other women, but that's your persona. Nevertheless, I can't be in a relationship with someone like that," she told him.

"Careful, you're starting to sound like I'm a distraction again," he said. He had that sinking feeling in his gut that no matter what he said, Lindsey was slipping further and further away from him.

"You are one. You have been great for motivating me to get back on my skis, and I'm not going to pretend I'd be as close to contemplating the Super G again without you, but at the same time we just don't fit together."

"We fit together just fine when you stop worrying and just let us enjoy our time together." He reached down and brushed his thumb over her lips, then clasped her chin in his palm. "What was it that spooked you this morning?"

She jerked away, as if his touch had singed her. "I'm not going to fight about this. I don't want to say anything else that is mean to you."

"Why not? Clearly you are okay with thinking them. So let's be clear here," he said, narrowing his eyes at her. "You are pushing me away for nothing other than your ego. Because you don't want to be the woman who is confident enough in herself and in her man to be with me. Be with that public image of me."

She nodded. "You're right. I'm not. Ego isn't my thing the way it is yours. I have tried to do this every way possible, but I keep coming back to the fact that you and I make no sense."

Except in his heart. "Lindsey, please. I can give up my sponsorship if it will make you stay with me."

She smiled at him, and his heart really almost broke. "No. That's not what I want. My fears stem from my own insecurities. I thought that maybe I could change that, but I can see now I haven't."

"You are that way because you've never let yourself care about another man before. Are you going to deny it?"

"No, because it would be a lie," she said stubbornly.

He thought it stemmed from his lack of a mother and how his father had never settled down. When Carter thought of forever— He didn't think of forever. The future was always changing, and as much as he thought at this moment that he needed Lindsey by his side, he was afraid he might be wrong.

17

WATCHING CARTER WALK away was the hardest thing she'd done in a long time. She was tempted to go after him and bring him back to her. In the end she knew she needed more from him than he could give.

But Carter had given her back something she'd lost. That confidence she'd used to be able to rely on. She grabbed her skis and went to the top of the Wasatch Range. The most difficult run serviced by the resort and the one she'd be skiing in two weeks' time for the charity event.

When she got to the top, she felt all of the crazy emotions that Carter inspired in her drop away. She stood at the top of the biggest run she'd dared to take since crashing out in Russia last year. Carter had made her realize a lot of things about herself, not the least of which was that she was no longer the woman she used to be.

But pieces of her still remained. She buckled her skis, pulled down her goggles and felt the breeze stir around her. The mountain was cold and very wintry today. Not the best day for a run, but she'd come up here, and nothing was going to stop her from taking it.

"Lindsey?"

She turned and saw that Carter was there. He'd followed her up the mountain. His hair was windblown, his shoulders broad as ever, and she had to turn away to keep from staring at him.

"What are you doing here? I thought we'd said all that we needed to." She was secretly thrilled to see him.

"We have, but I promised you I'd see you back on the slopes, and last night we said we'd take this run together. Despite what you think about me, I'm a man of my word."

She knew that. Maybe that was why she'd been pushing so hard for some sort of emotional commitment from him. She wanted some security in her life, and she had fallen in love with the one guy who was known for just drifting along.

"Thank you."

"You're welcome. It's a crap day, but I checked the mountain reports and there's nothing too dangerous. Are you ready for it?"

She wrinkled her nose. She wanted to say yes. Hell, she was going to say yes. "Of course. This is what I do."

"I'm glad," he said.

"This is part of who I am," she added, tilting her head up to meet his gaze. And she wanted to prove it to him. Downhill skiing was in her blood, part of her DNA at this point in her life. She'd spent more time on skis than off them.

"I thought you weren't sure anymore," he said wryly.

"I'm going to prove that I'm not only still a skier, but that I can beat you down the mountain."

He put his snowboard down and buckled his boots.

"I'd love to see you try. Hardly seems like a fair competition, though."

She knew what he was doing, but she didn't care. Driven by the need to prove him wrong, she put her poles in the ground and stumbled as a rush of fear swept through her body. It clouded her vision, and then all of a sudden images of her last tumble began playing through her mind. The crash that had left her broken and so flawed.

Not physically, she realized. No, she was hurting from the flaws the crash had revealed were inside her. The emptiness that was buried deep inside that she hadn't even been aware of until Carter had started to fill it up.

She looked at him. He had his goggles on as well, but he was watching her with that keen gaze of his, and she wanted so desperately to believe that he was scared for her because he loved her. But she didn't think for a second that was true. If she couldn't find the courage to say those words to him, how was the man who had more women running after him than anyone else going to say them?

"You okay?" he asked.

"No," she said. "I'm just realizing how not okay I am."

"I'll call the mountain patrol and we'll get down off the mountain," he said. "No shame in that."

She shook her head. "I have to do this, Carter. If I can't ski with you now, how am I going to be able to do it at the event?" Why had she even signed up for that stupid event? She should have run the other way instead of working with the team and acting as if she was okay. She wasn't.

"I'll just say that I'm not going to do it," he said. "You can say it wouldn't be fair for you to ski if I don't."

She looked at him, and all at once it hit her how much she loved him and how the words she wanted to hear might not mean anything when she was presented with the truth of his feelings. He did care for her. And the fact that he'd be the one to take the blame, make it seem like it wasn't her and her fear that was responsible, made her want to stop running.

And face life and her fears.

Fear number one: skiing. She had to do this, or she'd never be able to find happiness anywhere else in her life.

"Carter Shaw, you're a great guy. I'll have words with anyone who says different," she said. "But I have to do this. I have to stop hiding and running away from what I am."

"Are you sure?"

She nodded and turned back to look down the mountain. The breeze blew once again around her, and this time it swept away those doubts that had been lingering. She had her eyes wide-open, and the trail in front of her was one she'd taken many times before her crash. And had studied just as many times after it. She could do this.

Not only because she had to get back to doing what she loved, but because without taking this run, she had absolutely no shot at future happiness.

CARTER WATCHED LINDSEY take off down the mountain and let out the breath he'd been holding. In his life he'd never been afraid of a mountain. It just wasn't in his nature to see it as something to fear, but rather as something to conquer. But as he'd seen Lindsey on the precipice of taking her run, his heart had somehow climbed into his throat.

Talons of fear wrapped around him, and though he

knew she had the skills to safely make it down the mountain, he couldn't shake that fear. And it was at that moment that he realized he loved her.

He'd been "chasing" her from a distance, trying to protect his pride and safeguard his heart. Not because of any of the reasons he'd given himself before but because with Lindsey he knew his feelings were genuine. He had been giving her distance, hoping to keep himself safe, and now he was coming to realize how foolish that had been.

He should have held her closer to him while he'd had the chance. He should have held his tongue instead of pointing out her flaws to cover up his own. He should have told her he loved her instead of letting her believe that he didn't.

He jumped and swiveled and started his own run down the mountain. He knew as he did it that he needed to figure out how to get Lindsey back into his arms. Back into his life, where he'd really missed her. Because without her, he saw a future of more faceless women who were nice for a night but not forever.

It didn't take a genius to figure out that for him there was only Lindsey. And it had always been that way. She was the only woman that he'd ever really wanted, but he hadn't been ready for her until Sochi. And when she'd crashed, when she'd taken that devastating fall, everything had changed. He'd had no idea how to get back into her life until now.

She was ahead of him on the run, and as he watched her crouch low to increase her speed, he admitted to himself that her form was better than ever. She was good. Maybe better than she had been before because there was a new core of strength inside her from having lost it all and come back.

He wondered if while he'd been falling in love with her he had been giving her the very key to what she'd needed to move away from him. To go back to her old life where she wasn't surrounded by scantily clad energy drink girls or a man who couldn't control his temper.

It frightened him, but he pushed it aside as he hit a rough patch and barely caught his balance. He'd almost crashed out as she had last year. That shook him to the core. Was this how Lindsey had felt?

At the bottom of the run, he found Lindsey with her goggles pushed up on her head and a sheen of tears in her eyes as she looked up at the Wasatch Range. He got it. She'd reclaimed a part of herself that she'd thought was lost forever.

He hoped he'd made up for the teasing he'd done in Russia. She'd said he had nothing to do with her fall, but he'd never been able to shake his guilt. Not until this moment.

She was back. She'd ski again, and unless he'd completely lost his gut instinct when it came to other athletes, he was pretty sure she'd eventually be back to her old form. It was what she was meant to do. Not teach ski lessons to little kids at a luxury resort.

"Nice run," he said.

"Noticed you couldn't keep up."

"I gave you your space so that this victory could be all yours," he said.

She gave him a smile that cut through all the layers he'd been using to protect himself from her charms. It simply confirmed what he'd already figured out for himself. That he loved her.

"Still can't admit that I'm better on the snow," she teased.

"I can. I just don't like to," he retorted. "There's a big difference."

"I know." She hitched in a breath. "I'm sorry again for what I said earlier. I know that without you, I probably wouldn't have had the guts to do this."

"It's fine—I get it. We're oil and water, aren't we? We've never really been able to mix."

"I guess we are. So one more big battle and then you can go back to your life," she said.

"That's right. Back to California and training," he said. "Unless you want to try again?"

"Try again?" she asked, but he heard in her voice that she wasn't going to accept it. Perhaps it was his words spoken in anger but resonating still in her mind. And he understood that, because he knew he couldn't shake what *she*'d said.

He was a distraction. Distractions weren't welcome. God, how many times was he going to have to learn that?

"As a couple," he said, offering her an olive branch.

She shook her head. "I care about you, Carter, but it hurts too much to try to find a place for myself in your life."

"I could make room." For her he'd do it. Change whatever he had to.

"You'd resent me," she said. "I'd probably resent myself, too. I can't ask you to do that. Today as I was coming down the mountain I realized that I couldn't separate my skiing from my life, and I know it's the same for you and snowboarding."

Gazing down at her, he exhaled slowly and then trailed a finger down her cheek. "I guess I'm still just a distraction after all," he said. He knew he should tell her that he loved her. More than anything, he wanted to, but the words were stuck in the back of his throat. Fear was riding him hard, and he suddenly realized that he'd never felt afraid before because he'd never really had anyone that he didn't want to lose.

"You were never just that," she replied, stepping back. Then she took her skis and walked away.

He let her go, knowing that there was still unfinished business between them.

LINDSEY'S TEAM WAS in the best shape they'd been in since they'd started training. Lane Scott, the disabled American vet who was skiing on their team, was funny and inspiring. He was in his late twenties, maybe early thirties, and from his attitude it was hard to guess he'd lost both his lower legs to an IED in Afghanistan.

"I'm not sure that Tim should go before me. He's always flirting with the ladies and then they might miss my run," Lane said.

Tim, the fifty-five-year-old balding executive from one of the Park City resorts, just smiled over at them. "He's jealous."

"We all are," Bradley said. "But I agree with Lane. You should take the run after his and then we'll wrap it up with Lindsey. Carter's team been talking smack about beating our team, especially my wife, so I want to see them lose."

Lindsey hadn't realized how competitive Elizabeth was until the competition had gotten closer. At their daily breakfasts she'd listened to all sorts of good-natured ribbing from her friend. And to be honest, Lindsey had just been glad that Elizabeth hadn't brought up the argument with Carter. She'd asked one time if Lindsey wanted to talk and then let the subject drop when she had declined.

"Okay. Bradley, do you want to liaise with the other team and make sure we have all of our pairings in order?" Lindsey asked. "I'll be at the bottom when you come off your run and will radio up any changes in the slope to you guys at the top. That way you'll have up-to-date information before you take your run."

Everyone nodded. "Let's take our practice runs and do it like we will tomorrow. Since our regular guy isn't here today to man the radio at the top we will all take turns."

"I can't wait," Tim said. "My kids are going to be here tomorrow. My son got everyone in his school to donate."

"I'm really excited about the way the entire community has gotten behind us. I saw the poster in FreshSno, Bradley, that your graphic artists designed."

"Thanks. Those kids are awesome. Hard to believe they were wasting their talents painting graffiti on buildings."

Lindsey had heard about the kids Bradley had taken under his wing and turned from a life of punishable offenses into lucrative artistic careers. Speaking of changes… She'd given her notice at the resort, and at the end of the ski season, she'd be going back to training full-time. Her coach had wanted her to start right away, but she'd wanted to honor her commitment to the resort first. They'd given her a safe place to recover and now she wanted to pay them back with a win.

Plus, concentrating on winning had given her something to pour all of her emotions into over the past weeks. Never having been in love before, she'd had no idea how much it could hurt to care so deeply for Carter and know he was forever out of her reach. She missed him. He'd kept his distance since she'd walked away from him.

She didn't blame him for that. Because, in all honesty, she'd done the same thing. And it was easier to not see him than to catch small glimpses and be reminded that he wasn't hers anymore. Not that he ever really had been.

But she knew for a short while she'd had a good time pretending he could be hers. She had a selfie of the two of them on her phone from the day they'd gone diving in the crater, and she looked at it way too often. She'd almost deleted it but had been unable to because she wanted these small connections to him.

A part of her was tempted to go to him, to force him to see her because she knew that physically they still had that bond. But she had decided she wanted more from him than that. She knew if it was just sex, that bond would fade over time.

But it wasn't just sex. At least not where she was concerned.

But it was hard. She wanted to call and talk to her mother about it, but really, what would she say? Finally, she had a problem that had nothing to do with skiing. Even the joy she found at being able to ski wasn't enough to dull the ache left by Carter's absence in her life.

"Skier number one is in position."

The voice over the radio was deep and rich, and for a second she hoped it was Carter but then recognized it as TJ, one of the mountain patrol guys volunteering as a helper for their team on his day off.

"Thank you," she said.

"Go."

She hit the button on her stopwatch and waited for

Georgina to complete her run, but her mind wasn't on winning. It was on the feeling that dominated her thoughts whenever she was awake anymore. Where was Carter?

What was he doing?

Could she ever make him realize that he wasn't distracting her from her problems, but helping her to solve them? Because she knew that he had. Without Carter's quiet, steadfast support—taking her to places that weren't familiar, pushing her and challenging her at every turn, encouraging her to find her feet again—she would never have taken that run. And she just wanted one more chance to tell him that.

If she could get back on skis after that horrible crash, then why couldn't she do the same in their relationship? She'd been wrong to give in to her fears, and she wanted him back.

Now she knew she had to go and get him.

But winning back a man was something she had no clue about. She had an idea that her friend Penny would have some answers. She'd been a guest at the resort for two weeks during Christmas and had turned her holiday affair into happily-ever-after. If anyone could help her win Carter back, it was Penny.

18

CARTER HAD BEEN avoiding Lindsey, but being a coward wasn't his style so he'd decided to show up for her late-afternoon ski class. He liked the fact that he rattled her. He could tell by the way she kept losing her concentration with the kids. It wouldn't have been obvious to anyone who didn't know her as well as he did.

He was at the end of the line with two twin boys who looked like trouble and were barely old enough to be in school. They had freckles and matching bright red hair. Standing precariously on their skis, as though they were learning how to walk for the first time, they kept slipping back and forth and shoving each other whenever Lindsey's back was turned.

"Hello, boys," Carter said, stepping between the two of them to keep them from shoving each other. "I'm Carter."

"I'm Benji and this is Russ."

"Do you like skiing?" he asked, crouching to their level.

"No. I might if Russ would stop talking all the time. I can't hear what she's saying."

At this level Carter noticed that Benji had a hearing aid in one ear. "She's saying that you have to remember the skis are an extension of your leg. And that when you have them on you are gliding over the snow."

"How do you know?" Benji asked suspiciously.

"I've taken her class before."

"She mustn't be very good if you're back here again," Russ pointed out.

"She's very good," Carter said with a wink. "I like coming back because of her."

Russ scrunched up his face. "Girls are gross."

"Sometimes they are," Carter agreed. "Why do you keep shoving your brother?"

"He pushed me first," Russ said, looking up at him with wide blue eyes.

"Fair enough. But how about you two stop fighting and we learn how to ski?"

"I'm done pushing him now," Russ said.

Benji nodded in agreement. "Me, too."

Lindsey demonstrated a basic move. The kids slowly took turns doing it, going to the front of the group where Lindsey would watch them and give individual feedback. Carter moved around so he could go last. When he got up there she looked at him.

God, he'd missed her. She seemed tired, but happy. That made sense to him because he knew she was taking a lot of runs down the mountain to get ready to go back into training. He wasn't too proud to admit he'd asked Elizabeth about her.

"So you're going back to the team after the winter season is over," he said.

"I am. I figured out what I wanted for the rest of the year," she said.

"You did?"

"Yes."

"Care to tell me?" he asked softly. "I kind of have a vested interest since I started this year with you."

She looked at the kids who were watching them, waiting for Carter to take his practice time. "Not right now."

"And not later, either," he said, one corner of his mouth quirking up. "We both know that we're avoiding each other."

"We were until you showed up," she reminded him. "I can't talk right now."

It went against his nature to back down, so when the class went to the bunny slope he left, turned his skis in and went up to the lodge looking for a distraction. Something that would help him understand why he wanted that woman and why she kept freezing him out.

Granted, he knew that he hadn't shared his feelings with her and that it was hard to admit to falling in love. She acted as though it was a bad thing, but he knew she might find it hard to believe in him, especially since he hadn't admitted his feelings out loud.

"Hey, Carter! How's it going?"

He was surprised to see Will Spalding back at the resort. The dude had come over Christmastime and fallen in love with one of the other resort guests. They'd both been groomsmen in Elizabeth and Bradley's wedding.

"Not bad. What you are doing here?" he asked, shaking the other man's hand and sitting next to him at one of the lobby conversation areas.

"Penny wanted to spend our first Valentine's Day here and Elizabeth asked her to help plan the after-party for the charity event tomorrow."

"It's not too late for you to get in on it if you want to," Carter said.

"Get in on what?" Will asked.

Lindsey entered the lobby and walked over to the concierge desk with one of her young students.

Carter stared at her. That woman made him crazy. He wanted her—*loved* her—but he was hopeless at how to tell her. In his entire life there had never been anything he'd encountered that frustrated him more.

"You seem preoccupied," Will said.

"I'm just… Dude, I'm a mess. That woman is driving me nuts," Carter muttered. His snowboarding friends didn't get it. Had never had someone like Lindsey in their lives or they were still young and new to the sport so women weren't important to them. But Carter had moved on.

When he'd moved from amateur sports last year he'd signaled that he was ready to start his life after sports. And he was just now realizing it. He needed Lindsey in ways he'd never thought possible before, because it wasn't until he saw her standing by that kid in the lobby that he was struck with an image of her with *their* kid.

And that was precisely why he'd been running scared. It was time to stop running.

He started to get up to go over to her, but she was gone. She'd left the lobby. He looked around for her.

"Where'd she go?"

"I wasn't paying attention," Will said. "But I think she's having dinner with Penny and Elizabeth tonight. You could crash that."

Carter shook his head. He'd had enough of doing things with an audience.

DINNER WITH THE girls had seemed like a good idea when Elizabeth had first suggested it, but as she entered Elizabeth's house and noticed that Bradley and Will were nowhere in sight, she wasn't sure. The last time she'd been here had been when Elizabeth had tried on wedding dresses sent from California by Lindsey's dress designer cousin.

It was funny that her cousin had gotten all the romance genes and she'd gotten none of them. She should have flirted with Carter today, or heck, at least given him some sign that she still wanted him in her life. But instead she'd acted true to form, gotten scared and frozen him out.

She was like that ice queen in the Disney movie who always hurt the ones she loved by keeping them away. Her parents were a good example of that. She loved them, but they weren't close. Once she'd turned eighteen, she'd started living near her coach and never had time off to visit with them.

Her relationship skills were sadly lacking, and dinner tonight confirmed that until she had her second glass of wine and Penny turned to her.

"Rumor has it you've been hooking up with Carter Shaw," Penny said as she arched her eyebrows.

"Rumor?"

"Well, *Elizabeth*. But I want to know all the dirt," Penny replied. "You're pretty quiet for someone in the midst of a red-hot affair."

That was because, as usual, she'd doused the flames and there was nothing to tell. "I screwed up."

"What?" Elizabeth said, coming into the living room with a new bottle of wine. "What did you screw up?"

"Everything with Carter," Lindsey lamented. "I love

him but I can't find the words to tell him. He was at my class this afternoon and I just acted like I always do. Focused on skiing and pretended that I wasn't excited to see him."

Penny patted her hand. "Why did you do that?"

She glanced at Elizabeth. Her friend took sympathy on her and poured more wine into her glass.

"She called him a distraction and got into a huge fight with him in the restaurant," Elizabeth said, filling their friend in. "It wasn't pretty."

"No, it wasn't. But we sort of talked afterward and I realized that I'm not sure *I* wasn't a distraction for him. I'm just not good at relationships." She took a sip of wine, then went on, "Before this thing with Carter, I hadn't really had time for one, and now… Well, as I said, I screwed up and have no idea how to fix it."

"Sexy lingerie," Penny said, her eyes sparkling with mischief. "That will get his attention, and then afterward you just tell him all of that stuff you just told us."

Penny's idea had some merit. She could do the seduction thing. That part was easy between the two of them. "What if he doesn't feel the same way about me?"

"That's the risk you have to take when you fall in love," Elizabeth said gently.

Taking a sip of her own wine, Penny added, "And if he doesn't feel the same, isn't it better to know than to stay in the agony of what-if?" Penny had another valid point.

"Is that what you did?"

"No way. I just kept my guard up until Will stepped up and proved himself. I knew I loved him, but I had pretty much resigned myself to living with heartbreak for a while. But he made a big gesture," Penny explained.

"The dog? Everyone knows it was Fifi," Elizabeth said, poking her friend in the ribs.

"Well, not every guy has two great artists working for him so they can make a mural and hang it up for the world to see," Penny fired back, referring to the gesture that Bradley had made.

Was that what she wanted? A big romantic gesture so she knew it was safe to fall for him? Safe to tell him how she really felt?

She wasn't sure. Even if he did something like that, how would she be able to believe it? How would he believe it?

"Maybe I *should* do something to get his attention," Lindsey said, biting her lip.

"Lingerie," Penny reiterated. "Believe me, it works. Men can be brought around to your way of thinking once you have their undivided attention."

Lindsey swallowed, remembering New Year's Eve and how that night had worked out exactly the way she'd wanted it to. But since then she'd been struggling to figure out how to get him where she wanted him and not have to risk showing him any more of her weaknesses.

"It's different with us. Sex is easy. He thinks I was using him as a booty call and he's got all those scantily clad girls hanging around him," Lindsey said. But deep down she knew that wasn't true. She felt closest to him when he held her in his arms after they made love.

"Well, whatever the gesture, you better get moving. He told Will he's heading back to California on our flight in two days' time. And you've got the ski event and then my awesome party between now and then," Penny said.

"Maybe I could do something at the party?"

"Like what?" Elizabeth asked. "Given that the last

time you two interacted in public it felt like a nuclear meltdown, I think you need a plan."

"I do need a plan. I need something that shows him that I've finally figured out that we belong together."

"How?"

"Now, that's the million-dollar question, isn't it?"

She put her wineglass down and thought again of all the things Carter had done for her and how he'd taken time to help her learn to ski again when he was so busy... But he'd never been too busy for her. Carter had been there for her when she needed him most, and he had been there to catch her when she'd felt like she'd been stumbling around in the dark. Now it was her turn.

It was time to take the ultimate risk. To prove to Carter Shaw, once and for all, that she wanted only one thing for this year, and it was him.

CARTER AND HIS team were in high spirits, wearing the trademark green-and-gold Thunderbolt colors. The other team had gold with green accents, since Georgina and Stan had sponsored all the events. They were at breakfast in one of the ballrooms set up with two long tables on either side of the room. In the middle of the room were big, round tables draped in green or gold, depending on which team they had sponsored.

The tables in the middle were for the other big sponsors—resorts donating their instructors and their teams to help staff the event—and those tables were slowly filling. Carter stood to one side, smiling and joking with his team. Thunderbolt girls were moving around the room posing for pictures with the attendees.

They had their branded charity event logo on a big drape in the corner. It was set up with a backdrop of the

Wasatch Range so that guests could pose for a picture to appear as if they were skiing.

The wounded vets were very popular. Carter was pretty sure that Lane, Duke, Marsalis and Wynn hadn't had a minute to themselves all morning. Georgina and Stan were making the rounds, with Thunderbolt girls handing out beverages. Lars Usten had invited some of his old ski team cronies and they were all sitting at the head table.

Carter kept watching the room and knew that there was only one person he was looking for: Lindsey. But she had yet to show.

He worried about her, wondering if all the practice runs she'd taken had prepared her for this big run with so many people watching. Granted, it was nowhere near the pressure of the winter games, but this was the first time she'd be skiing in an event. It would bring back memories, he was sure of it.

"Hiya, Carter," Will said, coming up to him. He was wearing a pair of chinos and a button-down shirt. He looked as though he should be in the office instead of waiting to go out on the mountain.

"Morning. Nice event your— What is Penny?" Carter asked. He wasn't sure how to refer to her, but once people got out of high school it was hard to keep a straight face when calling them boyfriend or girlfriend.

"Well, girlfriend now," Will said. "But I have a surprise for her on Valentine's Day that should change that status."

Carter smiled and nodded at him. "Glad to hear it. I like you two."

"Thanks, buddy. You any closer to getting back in your lady's good graces?"

"Hopefully by the end of the day I'll have some good news for you," Carter said. "If not you can find me in the bar."

Will laughed as Carter had intended him to. Playing at being normal when he wasn't. He didn't have Lindsey and he didn't have a broken heart. He was still hopeful he'd win her back, but if he didn't, this would turn out to be the worst day of his life.

Yet he still was trying to play it cool so that no one could figure out how desperately he wanted and needed Lindsey in his life. He knew that nothing would be quite as good without her by his side.

He knew it. At the same time that knowledge paralyzed him. Made him unsure of what to do next.

But telling her was still a difficult thing. The words were hard, and he was so used to acting as though nothing mattered that now that something did he wasn't sure how to proceed. He had a plan, however, even though he had no idea if it would work.

He'd called his dad to ask for advice, but the old man had told him that if he'd had the answer to what women wanted he wouldn't have been married and divorced five times. But there had been no bitterness in his father's voice. And Carter had realized that every man had to find the path that worked for him. For Carter he couldn't see a path without Lindsey in it, which was why he was waiting for the right moment to show her what she meant to him instead of just finding out what he meant to her.

He had figured that out at three in the morning. Why was it that all the answers to his craziest ideas came to him then? He knew that tricking her into falling for him wasn't the answer, but it might be the vehicle to the answer.

Like the blindfold he'd used when they'd gone to the crater. It had turned out to be a sort of magic elixir to getting her to talk about all the things she usually kept locked away.

"You keep watching the door like you can make her appear," Will said, dragging him out of his thoughts.

"If only," Carter grumbled. "Life would be so much easier if she'd just do what I wanted her to."

"Really?" Will asked. "I've found that I don't always know what I want when it comes to Penny. She always surprises me, and it's better than whatever I planned."

He looked at the other man. There was an element of truth in his words. "I just want her to be here so I can make sure she's okay."

That was part of it. And then he was afraid he'd probably embarrass himself by going to her and pulling her into his arms. But that was what he wanted to do. He wanted to admit that he'd had enough of chasing her from a distance. To tell her that nothing was insurmountable when they were together. To say he should never have let anger motivate him into walking away from her.

Because he knew better than to let his temper control his actions. He was all prepared to say that…and more…but then Lindsey walked into the room with her long blond hair braided to one side and hung over her shoulder.

19

"I've got a new rule," Lindsey said as Penny led the way to the small stage that had been set up on the far end of the kickoff breakfast. The room was full, and she saw her teammates as well as the corporate sponsors... and Carter.

He stood by his team's table talking to Penny's boyfriend, Will. Penny had been sweet last night when she'd shared stories of how she'd been unsure of Will and how he'd overcome it. Elizabeth had bared her soul, as well. It had been humbling to realize that the other women had been in her shoes. She'd felt so isolated by her doubts.

"What rule?" Penny asked.

"No making important life decisions when I've had two glasses of wine," Lindsey said. Last night when she'd been trying to come up with the right gesture to show Carter how much he meant to her, it had seemed a good idea. But this morning, as she'd had her hair braided to match the Ice Queen image that was often used in the media to go along with articles about her, she'd started to have second thoughts.

"Do you want to spend the rest of your life in agony?" Penny said.

She noticed the pretty event planner wasn't afraid to go for over-the-top drama at times.

"Or without Carter?" Elizabeth asked, coming up on her other side.

"No, I don't. But this seemed like it would be a lot of fun last night and this morning… I'm scared."

Penny threaded her arm through Lindsey's left one, and Elizabeth did the same on her right. "We're here with you."

She smiled. She'd made good friends. It was one thing that she'd gotten from the past year. The time she'd thought was lost because she hadn't been skiing had turned out to be very valuable.

"Okay, I guess I'm as ready as I'll ever be," Lindsey said, bracing herself for whatever was about to come next.

"That's good, because it looks as if Carter has noticed you," Penny said. "Let's get this show on the road."

"What?"

"My mom used to say that every morning when it was time to leave," Penny said. "I don't get to quote her often enough."

Lindsey allowed herself to be distracted for a moment by Penny, but then searched out Carter. She found him, wearing his snowboarding outfit from the winter games last year, standing by his team table. And when their eyes met, she felt the courage that had been lacking in her until this moment.

She realized that once again she was drawing strength from him, and it felt right. He was her strength, and she needed to prove to him that he was more than a distraction. More than she'd labeled him, and that she was willing to take the risk and admit that she'd fallen for him.

Because she had fallen big-time for the bad-boy snowboarder.

And it was time to stop running from that love the way she'd stopped running from her fear of going down the mountain. She followed her friends through the crowded room, pausing to greet her team and tell them that she thought they'd win today.

The closer they got to the stage, the more her nerves almost got the better of her. But she had realized that nothing—not skiing again, not embarrassment—*nothing* scared her more than not telling Carter how she felt.

They got to the stage and Lars smiled at her and gave her the thumbs-up. She'd decided to take the entire big gesture thing and make it pretty gigantic. She glanced around the room and saw that everyone she'd talked to was in place, too. Bradley was standing by the sound system in the back of the room as she climbed up onto the stage dressed in her ski outfit looking like the ice queen as she took off her coat.

Penny and Elizabeth climbed the stage, too, and stood behind her. She cleared her throat as one of the techs handed her a microphone.

"Good morning, everyone," she said. The talking slowly died down and everyone turned toward where she stood at the front of the ballroom.

"First of all, thank you for participating in today's event and for volunteering your time and services for our event this coming November."

There was a round of applause and Lindsey took a deep breath.

"What many of you might not know is that this event was the brainchild of Carter Shaw."

She pointed to the corner where Carter stood. "There is probably a lot about Carter that you don't know, but the most important thing from my point of view is that he's…um…*not* a distraction to me."

She signaled to Bradley and heard the single drum beat before Cher started singing "The Shoop Shoop Song" and she lip-synched, "'Does he love me?'"

With Penny and Elizabeth dancing and shooping behind her, she met Carter's blue-gray gaze from across the room. Slowly she sang and danced her way over to him, weaving a path through the crowd as everyone clapped and turned to look at him, too.

She was more nervous about what he was going to do once she got to his side, but she felt alive and so in love with him at that moment that it really didn't matter. She wasn't going to be able to tell herself that he didn't know how she felt after this moment.

She stopped in front of Carter as the song ended with "It's in his kiss." She stood there for a minute and looked into his eyes.

"I wanna know if you love me so," she said quietly. She lifted her hands to his face, curving them against his cheeks as she went up on tiptoe and kissed him.

He stood there, his mouth rigid under hers for a moment, and she feared she'd made a huge mistake. But then she felt his arms come around her as he lifted her off her feet and spun her around in his arms.

"I do love you," he whispered into her neck. "I hope you felt it in my kiss."

CARTER FELT HUMBLED and happy and so damned glad that Lindsey had more courage than he did when it came to showing how much she loved him. He held her closely to him and never wanted to let go.

"Gorgeous, I loved that," he said with a big grin. Then he realized that everyone in the room was still staring at them. And if he'd learned anything from their last public discussion, it was that she preferred privacy.

He led her out of the room and down the hall to one of those little conversation nooks. He set her on her feet and gazed into her big brown eyes.

"Did you mean it?" he asked. He'd been alone so long. Felt so unattached to everyone else in the world that it was hard to believe she'd connected to him. That she loved him. Love wasn't something he'd ever prized until he thought he'd never have hers.

"Yes, I meant it. Would I sing that song and dance around the ballroom if I didn't?" she asked, still clutching his hand tightly.

She seemed to need his strength now that she'd made her confession, and he was more than happy to give it to her. "You do like the spotlight."

"Ha. You know I don't. Listen, I wore this outfit today because last year when I had my crash I felt like I lost everything. That my life was over. I retreated here and recovered physically, but mentally I had no idea how to fix myself.

"And then you showed up, teasing me and flirting and making me think about things that had nothing to do with skiing, but you woke me up. Shook me out of my icy state, and I'm not the Ice Queen anymore. You've made it so I can't be again. I really do love you, Carter." Tears shimmered in her eyes as she reached up and gently brushed a lock of hair off his forehead.

He brought his mouth down on hers, kissing her with all the emotion that he'd shoved deep down for so long. To hear her say those words and confess to loving him.

"Do you feel it in my kiss?" he murmured as he lifted his head. "I love you, Lindsey. I have never in my life been afraid of anything. I've never needed anyone. I'm happy to look for my next big challenge and move on, but the thought of leaving here without you by my side was unbearable." He cupped her face in his hands, one thumb gently caressing her cheek. "I wanted you to see me and know that last year when I dared and tried to claim a kiss, I was really coming after you.

"I was ready for our lives to stop being about competing on the snow and to make them more intimate. I can't live without you, gorgeous. I love you."

She smiled at him. "I was so nervous. But I wanted to prove how much you meant to me. I'm sorry for all the things I said. And how I acted at the ski lesson yesterday."

He sat on the couch and pulled her onto his lap, cradling her close to him as he stroked his hand down her back. He could hardly believe that she was his. At last, after all these years, he had the one woman he'd always been afraid to admit he wanted.

"I was pushing you, too. I didn't want to leave myself vulnerable. Admit I loved you before you did," he said. "Damn, gorgeous, you beat me to it today. I was planning to confess at the end of the events."

"Once again you are eating my dust," she said with a huge grin. "I couldn't wait. Skiing is important, of

course, but I needed to know where you fit in my life...
Well, that you'd be in my life at the end of the race."

He looked into those big beautiful brown eyes of hers
and felt a sense of rightness settle over him. "You have
me."

"Good. That doesn't mean I'm still not going to beat
you at everything we do."

"Uh, how do you figure you've done that?" he asked
drily.

"Um, poker, I won. World records—I've got two.
Your heart, I won again."

He'd won, as well...at poker and with her heart.

He cuddled her close and traced the line of her neck
down her arm and lifted her hand to his mouth to kiss
her palm before placing it over his heart. "You have my
heart, that is true. I have a world record, and I only compete in one event so that pretty much makes us even.
And...poker? I let you win."

She threw her head back and laughed. The joyous
sound echoing through the hall and through his empty
soul. "You let me?"

"That's my story, and I'm sticking to it," he said.

"If that's what you want to believe," she murmured.
"I want the man I love to be happy."

"I am."

She'd made him the happiest man in the world today.
Where he'd had doubt and fear and bottled-up emotion,
he now had Lindsey and her love. He knew that the
road for them wouldn't be traditional or smooth—that
just wasn't their way. But having her by his side was all
he'd wanted, and he could admit now that he was very
happy to have her by his side.

They both went back to their teams and competed in

their events. Carter felt a little nervous when Lindsey got ready for her run, but she did it like the pro she was and even beat him down the mountain.

But winning didn't seem as important now that he'd won her heart and had her by his side for today and the rest of their lives.

* * * * *

REQUEST YOUR FREE BOOKS!
2 FREE NOVELS PLUS 2 FREE GIFTS!

HARLEQUIN

Blaze®

red-hot reads!

Halloween

"My, oh, my, talk about temptation. A room filled with sexy SEALs, an abundance of alcohol and deliciously fattening food."

Olivia Kane cast an appreciative look around Olive Oyl's, the funky bar that catered to the local naval base and locals alike. She loved the view of the various temptations, even though she knew she wouldn't be indulging in any.

Not that she didn't want to.

She'd love nothing more than to dive into an oversize margarita and chow down on a plate of fully loaded nachos. But her career hinged on her body being in prime condition, so she'd long ago learned to resist empty calories.

And the sexy sailors?

Livi barely kept from pouting. She was pretty sure a wild bout with a yummy military hunk would do amazing things for her body, too.

It wasn't willpower that kept her from indulging in that particular temptation, though. It was shyness, pure and simple.

But it was Halloween—time for make-believe. And tonight, she was going to pretend she was the kind of woman who had the nerve to hit on a sailor, throw caution to the wind and do wildly sexy things without caring about tomorrow.

"My, oh, my," her friend Tessa murmured. "Now there's a treat I wouldn't mind showing a trick or two."

Livi mentally echoed that with a purr.

Oh, my, indeed.

The room was filled with men, all so gorgeous that they blurred into a yummy candy store in Livi's mind. It was a good night when a woman could choose between a gladiator, a kilted highlander and a bare-chested fireman.

But Livi only had eyes for the superhero.

Deep in conversation with another guy, he might be sitting in the corner, but he still seemed in command of the entire room. He had that power vibe.

And he was a superhottie.

His hair was as black as midnight and brought to mind all sorts of fun things to do at that hour. The supershort cut accentuated the shape of his face with its sharp cheekbones and strong jawline. His eyes were light, but she couldn't tell the color from here. Livi wet her suddenly dry lips and forced her gaze lower, wondering if the rest of him lived up to the promise of that gorgeous face.

Who is this sexy SEAL and what secrets is he hiding? Find out in A SEAL'S SECRET by Tawny Weber.
Available February 2015 wherever Harlequin® Blaze books and ebooks are sold!